FIGHTING OUT OF MOBBERLEY, ENGLAND

GB Hope

GB Hope

Fighting Out of Mobberley, England

A work of fiction by GB Hope ©

Published by Bronwyn Editions UK 2012

www.bronwyneditions.co.uk

ISBN: 978-0-9570745-1-4

Cover design by Jon Parris

Printed by Lightning Source UK 2012

A copy of this book has been sent to the British Library for legal deposit

Fighting Out of Mobberley, England

By the same author:

Who Do You Think *You* Are? You're My Henry Allbones

Queen of Spades

Stranger on Stranger

The Genie-alogy of Nathan Levy

GB Hope

To my Editor, Bernie Morris. It's a love, hate, love thing.

GB Hope

Acknowledgements

Thanks go to D for your generosity and unflagging backing of the project. And to think they said you were a small-minded miser.

GB Hope

FIGHTING OUT OF MOBBERLEY, ENGLAND

PROLOGUE

Michael Hester knew he was a total hypocrite. He disliked anything to do with Germany and the Germans: their football team, their stereotypical lack of humour and sun bed hogging, he found their major cities boring, their women unappealing. If he mentioned the war, during which they killed his grandfather at Caen in 1944, well, he just thought Germany should have been turned into the biggest farm the world had ever seen. He disliked anything to do with Germany except their cars, and currently owned two Porsches and a Mercedes McLaren. When he had started his textile business in 1983, he had driven a battered VW Beetle; within three years he was in a top of the range BMW. Recently, because of Jeremy Clarkson and the BBC programme, *Top Gear*, he had owned a Bugatti Veyron. But that had strangely disappointed him, somewhat, so he gave it away to the man who valeted his other cars.

He found himself in Germany, at Audi's test track north

of Wolfsburg, because Audi had the gall to refuse to bring their new version of the A1 over to his estate in Kent for a test drive. His fellow petrol-head, friend and lawyer, Nigel Gee, was with him for the visit. Normally, neither of them would look twice at any Audi below an A5, but this day was something out of the ordinary. They were in the hands of a bumptious German official from Audi whose name they had both let go in one ear and out the other. The blond man was in black slacks and a black polo-neck sweater and resembled Boris Becker, vaguely.

Boris had taken care of their needs since their arrival by private jet, offered them refreshments, shown an interest in the third Mrs Hester deciding to go on ahead of them to shop in Berlin. He had offered them an R8 supercar to have a go in as a warm-up, but Hester was happy to hang around the track until they were set up for the main event.

A shiny black A1 finally emerged with its track technicians, looking well-made, of course, but the smallest in the range and not very exciting to the two wealthy Englishmen. The A1 for 2016 looked even more aerodynamic than all the other cars that were inevitably going that way with the coming to the end of petrol and diesel powered vehicles. Hester and Nigel Gee wandered over with Boris to take a closer look. It was a left-hand drive model, not a snub to the English, but what Hester had requested.

'Do you want me to drive first, Herr Hester?' asked Boris. 'Or would you prefer–'

'I'll get straight to it,' answered Hester, ignoring being called Herr.

Boris climbed into the back. Nigel Gee took the passenger seat and Hester got behind the wheel. He seemed to swamp the driving seat. Not that he was fat, just a big man, his pink shirt open wide at the neck. His grey hair came forward onto an intimidating forehead that bore one or two scars from before the billionaire days.

Off they went in the A1 – Hester looked at Nigel Gee – pretty fucking underwhelming this. He took it up to sixty as they went along the isolated track through the woods. Boris, in the back, kept his own council. Hester was looking about the cabin. Where the handbrake should be was the main, exciting, part of the car. There was a small joystick sitting there, protected by a meshed metal box.

'Herr Hester,' said Boris, having waited patiently for the important part to begin, 'Currently we must slow to 20 mph before the box will open.'

Hester complied. 'Now?'

'Yes. Be very gentle, Herr Hester. Remember the instruction manual we sent to you.'

Hester pressed a switch and the box retracted off the joystick. There was a soft red button on top of the joystick which had to be engaged and held. This he did, looking again at Nigel Gee – pretty fucking amazing this!

Gently, very gently, Hester eased the joystick back, and slowly the nose of the Audi came up. Then, smooth as silk, but still sounding like a car, they were up, airborne, three or four feet off the ground.

'Remember,' warned Boris, 'if you take your foot off the accelerator in a normal car, that car will slow. If you take your foot off here, the car will slow and descend.'

Nigel Gee involuntarily giggled. Hester smiled at his lawyer.

'Not like a stone,' assured Boris. 'But let us keep everything smooth, yah?'

'Go higher,' urged Nigel Gee.

Hester did, but still stayed below the tops of the trees, giving the joystick a little turn to starboard, and then to port. With a great effort, he stopped himself from getting carried away and followed the straight road ahead.

'Absolutely fantastic!' Hester said over his shoulder, grinning broadly. 'I'll take one.'

'I shall certainly put you on the waiting list, Herr Hester.'

ONE

Lee was sixteen years old when his mother remarried in 2012, and he found himself in that not uncommon dilemma: should he take his new stepfather's name? But as that man's name happened to be Mr Lee, it did cause a few sleepless nights. Lee wanted to please his mother, he did get on very well with the new man, who was better than his real waster of a father, and, besides, Lee Pratt to Lee Lee wasn't all bad. For a time he started spelling his surname Leigh, but then he began working, with all the legal requirements that involved, so he just got into the habit of quickly explaining it away.

Lee Pratt had not done well in school, so Lee Lee was bored out of his mind with all his manual jobs by the time he was twenty: working in hotels in Chester, bars in Manchester and now, in 2016, a McDonald's in Liverpool. At least he was a supervisor – not that he ever told anyone that fact. Liverpool was because of his flame-haired Scouser girlfriend, Rachel, who he was quite into. They shared a flat in the Anfield area, although he was yet to notice Liverpool football club's ground. He was sure it was over there somewhere.

Rachel Rimmer also worked in McDonald's, and Lee liked trying to boss her about, but she was only part-time, being a student at Liverpool John Moores University. With a bit of luck, she would be able to get a good degree and look after him in later life. It was Rachel who spotted the businessman who was taking hours over a strawberry milkshake. Now, all of humanity must pass through a Liverpool McDonald's. Every imaginable kind of meeting, legal or illegal, or some need for time-killing takes place there, so there had to be a reason for Rachel picking this one man out from the crowd – and there was – he had arrived in a green Aston Martin DB9, was clearly rich, had a Cockney accent when ordering his shake and happened to be extremely hot. Lee noticed Rachel noticing the man and thought maybe his cushy future was not all that assured after all.

'I think he's assessing us,' Rachel said to Lee, to cover herself. 'He keeps writing notes after looking over.'

Lee looked across again. 'No, he's probably one of those sad gits who writes novels in restaurants.'

'Yeah, whatever.'

'Rachel, why don't you take your break now?'

'No, I'm not ready yet.'

'Oh, all right, then.'

One of Lee's older members of staff, a small ferrety-looking man, stopped at them in passing, raised an index finger in warning and said, with all seriousness, 'When I get home tonight I'm going to rip my wife's knickers off. They're killing me!' He burst out laughing at his own joke, then carried on with what he was doing.

Rachel looked at the man as if he were mad. Lee just grinned, then watched Rachel serve a customer. She was wearing tight black leggings below her uniform tee-shirt and she had a great ass. Glancing round at what all the other staff were doing, he caught sight of himself in some polished metal. He was a handsome man, in great shape. Maybe he could have been a little taller and muscular. Rachel stood two inches above him when she came back over.

'Go and ask him what he's doing,' she told him.

'Don't be silly.'

'Can I ask him?'

'Again, don't be silly.'

'No, officially, Lee. Can I? He's bugging me for some reason.'

'Well, I suppose, if you engaged a customer in polite conversation you could ask him what the fuck he thinks he's playing at.'

With that she was away. Lee watched her take a twisty route across the restaurant before she was in front of the man. He looked up and smiled, and they started chatting. And the chat continued, with Rachel putting a hand on a hip (the sign she was deep in thought) then she re-did her ponytail within her baseball cap. And still the talk went on. When she actually sat down, Lee took the hump and went over there.

Another Londoner was Up North at the same time as the man in Liverpool. She was also in a restaurant, a Beefeater-type establishment, in the city of York. She was sipping mineral water at the bar, while perusing an unappetising menu. The parameters of the job she found herself engaged on had stated Yorkshire, so she could have been anywhere in the county, but she had chosen York because she had recently seen a documentary on the History channel about the city. She'd had a walk around, seen the old walls and some of the quaint streets, bought a mug with an image of York Minster on it, and greatly liked the whole place. She ignored all the tourists, because she was only interested in local people.

She opened the leather folder on her lap. She knew what she had to do – it was just so out of the ordinary that she wanted to double check what her exact instructions were. The couple she'd followed in there seemed to fit the bill for the first part of her mission. There were three others: a thirty-something single man who should seem to have practical skills, maybe a joiner or a roofer; a single, attractive twenty-something dark-haired woman with a strong Yorkshire accent who resembled the actress Claudia Cardinale. Before leaving London she had googled Claudia Cardinale and carried a photo in the folder. Good luck with that one, she thought. Finally on the list, a British Asian doctor of either sex. Good luck with that one, as well.

The couple were clearly not tourists, by the way they chatted with the husband and wife proprietors. They were in their early forties, in smart casual, the woman with short bobbed black hair and the man greying but fit-looking, tanned, as if he worked outdoors. Maybe he was a roofer and she could kill two birds with one stone. She let them order first and choose where they wanted to sit. Then she approached the till, ordered and paid for a cheese salad sandwich and indicated where she would be – within speaking distance of the couple.

She listened in to their conversation, which was mainly work based; no mention of children, which was good. The man slightly raised his voice once or twice, which made her hesitate a little. She was to get a couple, not a bickering couple. She decided to get in there before any arriving food complicated matters, and begged their pardon, could she speak to them for a moment?

A colleague of the man in Liverpool and the woman in York had perhaps the easier assignment; London and the South-East were his designated catchment areas. With no intention of squandering his travel allowance, he had already discounted going outside of London and, having sat for half a day in the office trying to get his head round the bizarre task in the first place, had decided to go home to Clapham to fill his quota from there. On his list he had an attractive, single black woman without complicated family connections, whatever that meant; an adult male of any age under sixty, who was allowed to be foreign if need be, although not German; and a sixteen-year-old white English boy without obvious prospects or caring family. He had the last one nailed down already – his nephew, Will. Will's family didn't like the lad at all and would be happy to be shot of him for a while. He intended to split the big money with Will, but hadn't gotten round to telling him yet. The man he could find, no trouble, but he currently didn't know any black people. Then a spark of inspiration reminded him that his kid sister had a pretty black friend. From the kitchen of his flat he called his sister straight away and, although she sounded like she was engaged in something disgusting with her boyfriend at the time, got all the information he needed.

The black girl was called Cozzie, and she was a model – *Cozzie? Are you winding me up? No, I'm not. Piss off, I'm busy* – who lived in nearby Battersea. He rang Cozzie straight away, dropped his sister's name into the conversation and said he had a business proposal to put to her. They arranged a meet for that evening. That she wasn't busy with modelling work was a good sign.

Then he was stuck again. He decided to walk round to his brother's house and try to find nephew Will. Maybe the man he needed would present himself in some shape or form without having to make any effort.

As he was not currently in employment or education, Will happened to be hanging about in his front garden, together with his gormless mates, two broken washing machines and an overflowing skip that never seemed to get paid to be taken away.

Will offered his uncle a can of Special Brew, which he declined. They moved away from the group.

'Shouldn't you and your mates be out rioting somewhere?' he asked.

Will was then given a snippet of what the deal would eventually be – no reason to terrify the boy straight off the bat. Good money was mentioned, and free accommodation, getting away from London for a while. Basically, it was like an arse over tit Borstal. No, no, that just confused Will. More of a club getaway, he was told, team bonding in isolation. Will looked blankly at his uncle, who slapped him on the arm and told him it would all make itself clear in the end.

He met Cozzie that evening in a wine bar on Battersea Rise. She was much fitter than he remembered, very thin and tall with sleek straight hair. For some reason he had pictured her with a huge afro. He tried to make conversation, while puzzling over whether her lips were the sexiest he'd ever seen in his whole life. Once she had a large drink out of him, Cozzie told him she was desperate for money, that he should come straight to the point, and that if it didn't involve animals then she was in.

GB Hope

TWO

There was a fourth and final member of the team with a list of specific people to find, and he had struck lucky. For some reason, New York or the East Coast was his area, and he only had to pick up a young woman from that city and an old man from any nearby state. He arrived by British Airways with every intention of having a jolly good week's holiday in the Big Apple. He'd been there once before, Christmas shopping with the wife. At the moment she was *the* wife because they had argued over household spending while times were so tough, or more accurately her failure to control household spending while times were tough, prior to his departure. She would have calmed down by the time he got back to London and become *his* wife again.

As he took a cab to the hotel, with the window down amid the humid New York summertime, he had no idea how to accomplish his mission. Perhaps the woman could be found in a bar, after trying it on with twenty others first. But the man? How to approach the man with such a crazy deal? Hotel staff, low paid, maybe not even American, looking for someone to offer them the Dream. It might not be that difficult after all. He had a lot of dollars to flash around, he was in a five-star hotel, and looked the part. That should ensure he was at least listened to.

In the end, he didn't even have to leave the hotel. There was a bar downstairs which he went to after his dinner. His English accent got him into conversation with a number of women, some holiday makers, some businesswomen. He was patient and never got to the crux of the matter, dropping hints that he was looking for a person, letting them think he was a casting director. He enjoyed the chat even when the lady in particular had disqualified herself by being from out of town. For a moment he was doing so well he thought of postponing his work and simply getting off with whoever accepted his best offer. Megan from Colorado was a definite goer.

Cathy from Buffalo brought him back in line. Buffalo was New York State – surely, that was fine. She was a twenty-four-year-old slim brunette, in New York City to visit old friends, who were late. She was intrigued by the Englishman with his vague business talk, that he was in from London to offer £100,000 to the right person. It was strange. It was different. No, it wasn't kinky. Sure, he could talk on until her friends came.

He had Cathy signed by the end of the week. It took a good vetting by her friends, three expensive meals, a more expensive trip up to speak to her only living parent in Buffalo. Cathy was single, very recently heartbroken, in fact, the reason for the trip to New York. She was crazy about the environment, loved England without having been there (Prince William just did it for her) and the money blew her mind.

Just when he thought he would leave New York with only

one target completed, the hotel liftman, Madesio, finally said yes. He had been propositioned twice every day that week. He had kept giving the "you're a crazy Englishman" smile. Madesio was a New Yorker of Puerto Rican descent. Forty-two years of age was probably stretching the "old" criteria, but he had clearly had a hard life. Madesio was even more delighted with the hundred grand than Cathy was.

Lee wasn't sure what was upsetting him more, his girlfriend meeting the Londoner behind his back after her last shift, or what she had just told him. He stood in the doorway to their bathroom, in the flat in Anfield, tapping his foot and chewing a fingernail as he stared at her in the bath. By comparison, Rachel was chirpy, checking her teeth in the mirror which sat on top of the laundry basket, waiting for him to get his head together and stop being stupid.

'Lee, it's a brilliant idea.'

'He wanted you, not me.'

'Well, he needed a fella as well, so I've done him a favour. And, besides, you haven't got exams like me. It'll set us up, big time.'

The *big time* came out sounding proper Liverpudlian.

'Rachel, it's mental.'

He watched with his usual fascination as she had a brief shave of her long legs.

'You've done this kind of thing before,' she reminded him. 'That drug trial in the Manchester clinic.'

'That was two weeks. This is six fucking months!'

Her ablutions complete, she stood up, taking the towel he offered to wrap her body in. 'Lee, babe, it'll be an experience.'

'What, like going to prison?'

She stepped from the bath and moved up close to him. 'New people, tucked away somewhere nice, just like *Big Brother*.'

'I hate *Big Brother*.'

'And think of the money you'll save on bed and board. I could take in a lodger while you're away.'

'Holy shit! Who are you going to take in, Rachel, this London geezer?'

'Now you're just being a dick.'

She departed for the bedroom.

'I'm being a dick?' he asked, following.

'Right, are we going out, or what?'

'Sorry, I ain't, frankly, in the mood to go out.'

The towel was loose, being worked all over her body. Her slick breasts were being moved around, probably deliberately. She drifted near to him again. He played with her hair, all piled up on top of her head. She began nibbling his right earlobe. He was amazed how easily he calmed when she did something like that.

'We could stay in,' she purred.

'But you're all spruced up.'

'Only for you.'

'Rachel, stop it.'

'Why?'

'Let's cut to the chase on this thing. Give me one serious reason why I should meet this guy.'

The towel had succumbed to gravity between their two bodies. 'One hundred thousand pounds.'

Our Man in Clapham found his last person by simply talking to his Romanian window cleaners. He had watched them for a while from a stool in his kitchen, as he was eating his muesli, considering their technique to be a little sloppy, thinking of suggesting they should swap their shammy leathers for some of those squeegees. Alexandru, or Alex, was the single man of the trio, totally sick of London (he'd foolishly expected it to be full of English people). He was ready to get rich and get out and jumped at the chance of being signed up, without giving it much thought. He gave the impression that he would have been up for The Great Train Robbery.

So, our man thought, what did he have? Stupid nephew, Will, black model, Cozzie, and Alex, the useless Romanian window cleaner.

The Yorkshire contingent was filled easily enough, as it turned out. The woman from London did in fact kill two birds with one stone by going into a Doctors' Surgery and asking for an appointment. The receptionist with the broad Yorkshire accent had luscious brown hair and a pretty, pale complexion. She didn't look very much like Claudia Cardinale, apart from her striking black eyes, but by a bizarre co-incidence her name tag had her pinned as a Claudia. She was quite feisty, judging by the way she dealt with two very unhappy patients in the queue.

In to see the doctor, by the luck of a cancellation, she started by saying he might want to have her committed on the spot and she apologised profusely for wasting his time, but she told him her problem anyway. The doctor, a handsome, friendly type, laughed, thought about it for a moment, then lifted a hand from his crossed legs, pointed at her and said, 'There is my friend, Dr Afridi. He's just left a GP's position in Knaresborough. He could be your man. Shall I call him for you?'

While waiting for an answer, she went after Claudia, who had to be tracked down to a cigarette break outside the main entrance. It was another sign of her strong personality, as smoking in public places had been banned in 2015. Asking for a light helped to start conversation, and complimenting Claudia on how she handled the unruly patients had them both laughing. When Claudia asked if there was a problem with the doctor being able to see her, it opened the way to broaching the subject.

Flabbergasted, but not dismissing the idea out of hand, Claudia went back to finish her shift, promising to continue the talk in a couple of hours.

The final person on the list, a male, single, manual worker of some kind, almost came out of thin air, literally, as she was finishing her cigarette. She was loudly wolf-whistled by a builder across the road. She was straight over there, giving it her best sexy walk – *work it, baby, work it* – cheekily challenging the man as his mates looked on from scaffolding. She gave him the offer straight out. He told her she was taking the piss. She tried again, hinting that his building job was slave labour and liable to be taken away in the current economic climate, and that he should listen to what she was saying. He told her she was joking again. She told him he was a moron. He told her she was a fucking bitch. She walked away with her middle finger up in the air.

She decided to get petrol while waiting for the doctor. She drove her white Audi A3 to the filling station up the road, looking at the prices as she pulled in: Unleaded £1.96 a litre, Diesel £2.08 a litre. Two years of refinery blockades, army interference and the general fury of the motoring public had failed to stop the steady astronomical price climb. Now, apathy and misery summed it all up – the country had long since gone to the dogs.

With a packet of Cheddars and a bottle of mineral water, she returned to the surgery. Claudia waved her over with a note from the doctor. It was an instruction that she should telephone a Dr Afridi on the provided number. She sat down and called the man immediately. Dr Afridi was in Leeds and sounded desperate over the mobile to see her that evening. She took his address and agreed a general time to get there. Then she settled in again to wait. Claudia looked over sporadically throughout the rest of the afternoon.

She was losing the will to live when Claudia was finally there in front of her, her bag over her shoulder, ready to go. She thought Claudia had a sensational figure, with a short skirt and bare, tanned legs, and wondered if that was a good thing or not for the adventure ahead of her. Claudia suggested a nearby pub where they could finish their chat, reconsidered because it was bound to be full of builders by then, but was assured it would be fine.

Inevitably, the builder given the bird earlier in the day, happened to be in the pub. He approached her and Claudia at the bar, but with a broad smile on his tanned face. Apparently, away from his mates, he was ready to listen to offers. His name was Henry. She insisted on buying him a drink. As she waited for the bartender, she took in Henry's firm, muscular body under his checked shirt – he wasn't exactly unattractive but she felt she wouldn't want to spend any great length of time locked away with the man. She glanced at her watch. It might turn out to be a very productive day – she had an hour before driving over to Leeds to see Dr Afridi.

She decided there was no need to rush, to make absolutely sure of these two - Dr Afridi was a sure thing.

THREE

Lee slept with Rachel, slept on the problem, slept with Rachel again in the morning, and saw the immense benefit of what was on offer. With or without her, in six months time, he would be minted, a mini-lottery winner who could stop working for a while, train to be something else, travel a bit.

He and Rachel met the London man in a different Liverpool McDonald's, because it was the first place Lee thought of over the phone. Immediately, there was an offer of 200k on the table. Why didn't they both go? Do the exams later in the year. Just pretend not to be a couple, even start dating while the thing was going on. Wouldn't that be fun?

Rachel wasn't having any of it. Lee was all the man was getting. They talked over hamburgers and strawberry shakes. Lee felt like swearing – it was all good, bonkers but good, he couldn't fault it, but it was asking so much of him. It was a life changer for the normal kid from Cheshire.

They had a couple of weeks before he was to be taken to London – it was not, *expected in London*, but picked up and chauffeured down there. Because he liked and respected his boss, he didn't just quit on the spot, but worked out some notice. In true "have a blow-out before the sentencing date comes round" style, Lee enjoyed his favourite Indian meal six times in a row, and he and Rachel even had a day out in Rhyl in North Wales so he could take a look at the sea. From there, they went to stay with his mother and stepfather for a couple of days, without mentioning the plan to them at all. Then they spent what time they had left together: basically, shagging.

The Londoner in Liverpool sat in his Aston Martin, looking at the Anfield football stadium, assessing his success so far. His criteria had been to get a Liverpudlian woman and a Liverpudlian man. He'd achieved the second part by default – well, he'd got a man while in Liverpool, at least. Now, all he had to do was get that original woman, as well as another sixteen-year-old girl from the city.

He'd decided he didn't like it on Merseyside. What was the client's obsession with these people, anyway? He was thinking about getting home, but then told himself to focus, think of his commission. Liverpool fans in their red shirts passing by made him think of his beloved Tottenham Hotspurs. He grabbed a newspaper from his passenger seat and flicked to the sports pages. As he thought, Spurs were playing a pre-season friendly at Blackpool the following night. He was too close to miss that, so would retire to his hotel, drive up the coast tomorrow. His current girlfriend happened to be a dental assistant, so he would wind her up with a present of Blackpool Rock. As for the job, no need to panic, he told himself, he had all week.

It rained all the following day, so close to the Irish Sea.

He lazed around his hotel, before doing some shopping, glancing at every woman who passed him, but it was like looking for a lay-by on a long car journey – by the time you'd decided to pull over, you had gone by. Early afternoon, he drove up to Blackpool, disappointed not to be able to see the tower from way off because of the weather. Some Northern monkey gave him rambling directions to Blackpool FC's ground. He found a place to park and took a walk along the windy promenade, happier seeing all the Tottenham shirts milling around. The sea looked angry and the tower seemed too far away. He headed north, buying a hotdog, some gold Elvis sunglasses and a small piece of rock. After the hotdog, he spent a happy hour in an amusement arcade. After that he was nearly at the tower – might as well go up it. But he baulked at the extortionate entry fee, so found himself back on the Prom, looking at a droopy-headed horse and its yellow carriage. That wasn't something he was going to do.

He crossed the road to get a better look at the sea. Heavy clouds prevented him making out the horizon. Then a squall of rain came in, forcing him to scuttle to a bus shelter. He realised it was already occupied by local youths; hooded and demonic, with nothing whatsoever to do with their time. When he retired, he intended buying a house overlooking the sea, anywhere in the world but Blackpool.

The nearest hoodie turned to him. Here we go, he thought, this is their bus shelter. Move on or get stamped in the head. But the person didn't speak to him, just looked at him. He realised with a start that it was a girl, that the face was lovely, stunning even. It was only slightly foreign-looking, as if she had some Middle-East in her genes. Then, as if reading his mind, she violently threw the hood back off her head, showing black hair pulled into a ponytail. In the gloomy atmosphere, the whites of her eyes were shocking in their brightness. There wasn't much to her: a delicate waif of about sixteen. If she suddenly said "orl-right, mate?" then he was in with his second Liverpudlian.

Then he realised how ridiculous this part of his mission was. How could you coerce a sixteen-year-old girl, with parents, family and police around? He felt extremely creepy even being there in the bus shelter and looked for the rain to have abated. He was out of luck. The girl smiled a beautiful smile, not at him; she had earphones in and something had pleased her. He was about to leave anyway and get drenched when she popped one earphone out of place and told him she was listening to Paul Weller. That puzzled him enough to pull a face. Paul Weller was superb, of course, but not what he would have expected her to be listening to.

He asked how old she was? Sixteen.

Did she live in Blackpool? At the moment.

Who did she live with? Foster parents.

What was her name? Leila.

He didn't get to see Tottenham play Blackpool, and he didn't get his other Liverpudlian woman, either. He spent the rest of the week with Leila, not as a predatory twenty-six-year-old male but more like a long-lost friend. Half an hour after the bus stop meeting he was feeding her in a café, and then he paid to take her into the Pleasure Beach until it went dark. The following day he picked her up from the house she was living at, thankfully without meeting her foster parents, and took her up the tower, a first for both of them. In tee-shirt and jeans, without the hoodie and the sullen friends, she came across as less dysfunctional. Still, there wasn't much conversation and there lingered suspicion that one crossed word would send her flying off the handle, but she laughed at his bad jokes, expressed a liking for the car. He managed to learn that her mother was in prison, that she did have brothers but didn't know where one of them was, while the other was overseas with a security company. He did send her money, she said. Jesus, he thought, one of her brothers was a mercenary.

In sunshine she was even cuter, with a few freckles over the bridge of her nose. With her freshly washed hair and delicate perfume she was good enough to... *stop it!* He agonised over how, or in fact whether, to tell her the proposition. She was perfect for it, she ticked all the boxes, but he wanted to do the right thing by her. He laughed – he'd be writing a mission statement next.

On the way to Blackpool Sea Life Centre, she asked if he wanted to have sex with her. *Sorry, what? No, you're all right.* Quickly he asked where she was from. He expected something exotic, but she said Southport, down the coast a little.

The next day she asked to be taken clothes shopping; she had a little money from her brother. He wanted to tell her that she didn't need to buy any new clothes, she would have her free pick soon, but he took her into the city of Preston anyway, and paid with his own credit card. It was there, in a Subway sandwich shop, that he told her the reason why he was up north. She continued to chew in an un-ladylike fashion, but she leant forward and her eyes looked at him as if she was playing a pool shot. He wondered if he could adopt her, while at the same time being able to look down her top and see most of her small breasts.

Eventually she said okay. He assured her he would explain it all, and that she had nothing to worry about. All she asked was that he kept her brother informed. He agreed, but put down his sandwich, no longer hungry at the thought of telling a mercenary what he'd got his sixteen-year-old sister involved in.

At his sprawling mansion, just outside Sevenoaks in Kent, Michael Hester was getting dressed in the master bedroom. He was shaving with his travel-shaver, to get himself used to it. Although he looked like a bull of a man, he was surprisingly nervous and couldn't wait for things to start. It was the reason he had arranged that day's little outing, and why, when he craned down to look through the window, he could see his lawyer friend Nigel Gee's BMW coming up the long drive.

Hester had bought and worn-in a new pair of Rockport boots – he would be putting those on. His clothes were chosen for the big day and the third Mrs Hester, while in Berlin, had bought him a leather man-bag which would prove useful for his personal items. He'd already visited his dentist and doctor that week – yet still the time dragged.

He met Nigel Gee by the pool, together with a capable man he'd used before, by the name of Frankie King. They all sat down around a pitcher of something fruitily alcoholic that his manservant had set out for them.

'Are we good to go, Frankie?' asked Hester.

Frankie King wore a stern expression because of the reputation and the money he was facing. 'We are, Mr Hester. The location is set and completely sealed. Local press have bought the reason for the delays and why the opening date has been pushed back: building regulation problems, the overall economic climate, etc. Of course, all the shops have accepted the top secret story about the major gas fault, and have accepted your compensation packages. They don't want to pressure you and risk the future of the venture when it does open next year. We're all booked for the London hotel meeting and subsequent evening transfer to the location.'

'Very good. Now, tell me about the people.'

'We have twelve, including a married couple. Your requirements as to gender, ethnicity, what have you, have been followed. There was just a slight failing on Merseyside. Two out of three there, I'm afraid. The person responsible has been disciplined. But I'm sure you'll be pleased.'

'What do you mean, disciplined? Do you mean sacked? Reinstate the person forthwith and make sure they are fully paid. I knew it was a difficult task, and I'm in such a great mood. There should be nothing negative about this event.'

'I'll see to it straight away, sir,' said Frankie.

Hester relaxed back into his chair, indicating for Nigel to pour some drinks.

'You'll both stay for lunch, of course. Then we'll set off.'

Mrs Hester put in an appearance, with two equally attractive girlfriends, all in daring swimming costumes.

'I'm sorry, darling,' said Mrs Hester. 'I didn't know your

guests had arrived.'

'That's all right, sweetheart. The pool's all yours. We're going in for lunch, then we'll be out of your hair.'

Mrs Hester smiled, then the three women went into the pool with various standards of dives. 'Bring your drinks, gentlemen,' said Hester, leading Nigel Gee and Frankie King away, the latter dragging his heels.

After a leisurely lunch, the three men walked over to Hester's large brick garage, converted from a stable block. Hester indicated a white Audi A1 to Frankie King. 'I thought we'd go in that one, Frankie. What do you think?'

Frankie King looked at the A1. He shot a glance at a grinning Nigel Gee. He thought it a quality car but didn't fancy being squeezed into the back of it for the long journey they had ahead of them.

'Only joking,' said Hester. 'We're taking that Porsche there.'

Now you're talking, thought Frankie King, assessing the black, Porsche Panamera. It sat there, spotless, looking as if it had just had one of those £1,500 two-day valets.

'Fabulous motor, Mr Hester,' said Frankie King, as he was invited to get into the back.

Nigel Gee, answering a call on his mobile phone, took the passenger seat and Hester drove them away at speed through his extensive grounds. He slowed briefly to see if he could spot his horses out in their paddock, then went through the ornate gateway and pulled out onto the road.

It was about an hour into their journey north, touching 100 mph whenever possible, when Hester turned to Nigel

Gee. 'I'm quite disappointed with this car, you know, Nigel.'

'So am I, now you mention it. It does seem a bit limited, in some way.'

In the back, a tad nervous with the speed they were going, Frankie King puzzled over their negative comments about the fantastic Porsche.

They stopped just the once at a service station, where Nigel Gee took over the driving, then they hit South Yorkshire, finding their way towards Leeds. Just before the motorway ended, they were picked up by a black BMW, which tailed them for half a mile before overtaking and flashing its hazard lights. This was their pilot to follow into the city centre.

The BMW led them all the way to a business park where both cars pulled up. Hester and his party got out to stretch their legs. A smartly-dressed man stepped out of the BMW and spoke to Nigel Gee.

Nigel Gee went to Hester. 'Just around the corner. We're right on time. He's due any minute.'

The three of them followed the man in the suit. He indicated the steps to an office building, then wandered further on - he gave the impression of liking the dramatics of his profession. They had to wait a few minutes. Frankie King had managed a cigarette when they stopped on the motorway; he could do with another one, but decided against it, especially as Nigel Gee pointed out the arrival by taxi cab of a middle-aged British Asian couple – the man looking distinguished with a neat, greying beard and wearing a light, grey suit. The smaller lady was in traditional Pakistani attire, with a sternly worried expression on her face.

'Here's our good Dr Afridi, for his hearing.'

'Remind me,' said Hester, 'he was suspended, why?'

'Repeatedly failing to spot cancer in a patient.'

Hester raised his eyebrows. He watched the couple ascend the steps slowly, pause to gird themselves, then disappear inside. Hester clapped his hands together, ready to move on. 'He'll do for me. I like the look of our Dr Afridi.'

Nigel Gee continued with the driving duties, for the thirty minute burn up to York, where on the A64 just south of the city they were collected by another BMW, which guided them in.

The next place they stopped at was the car-park of Claudia's doctors' surgery. Frankie King lagged behind, looking for a chance to have a quick fag, but he was waved to join them by Hester. They walked into a fairly busy reception area and took up a position on the far wall. Nigel Gee pointed out Claudia behind the reception desk.

'She's called Claudia?' asked Hester, enthralled.

Nigel Gee checked the details he had with him. 'She is, yes.'

So that was the Claudia Cardinale one, thought Hester. He wasn't the slightest bit disappointed that she was beautiful in a different way.

'Very good,' Hester said, after a moment of watching Claudia. 'On we go. We'll eat in Liverpool.'

And have a fag, hopefully, thought Frankie King, trailing them out. His mind was taken off his nicotine dependency by being handed the keys to the Porsche.

'It's a shame,' Hester was saying, 'I would have liked to

have seen York Minster while we were up here. But, never mind, onwards!'

Frankie King drove them back in the direction of Leeds, absolutely loving the Porsche. They joined the M62 there for the trip over the Pennines. At one stage he touched 96 mph - at least that was what the traffic policeman quoted as he wrote out the speeding ticket.

He took it easier from then on, with Hester and Nigel Gee seemingly content as passengers, with two fifths of their targets having been met. There was just Lee to see in Liverpool, working his final shift, then home to London to check out Leila and Cozzie.

Yet another BMW found them before they came off the motorway at Liverpool. Frankie King followed it for ten minutes or so until it pulled into a McDonald's restaurant car-park.

'Use the drive-thru,' said Hester. Frankie King looked at him; surely they were going to stop. 'I want to look through the hatches, then we can pull over to eat.'

In the queue, Nigel Gee strained to see through the Plexiglas windows, until he finally called out, 'There's our guy.'

Hester watched Lee until he moved out of sight again. They placed their order, Hester handed over the money to pay, and the Porsche went over to park in a bay.

After their fast food meal, they split up to have a walk about and savour the Merseyside air, to visit the Gents and to finally have that cigarette in Frankie King's case.

'Liverpool, eh?' said Frankie King to himself, as he looked over the part of the city visible to him from the car-park. 'Not the prettiest place I've ever seen.'

Hester took a closer look at Lee whilst inside the restaurant. With an imperceptible nod of his head to himself, he returned to the car.

Rachel Rimmer had noticed the Porsche Panamera, but the three men were of no consequence to her.

Hester bombed south back down the M6 towards The Midlands, despite a little late afternoon fatigue setting in. At the services on the M40 near Oxford they were met by yet another BMW, but this one provided someone to take the Porsche off their hands, while they fell into the BMW, to be taken on to London.

Frankie King, too junior to have been fully briefed on the day's itinerary, enjoyed the soft drinks in the BMW and the more leisurely pace, finding himself surprised but pleased when they turned up at a cinema multi-plex. With a bit of luck, Hester wanted to see a movie, and so he could catch forty winks. He was disappointed, they were just there to linger about in the foyer – with not even any popcorn to be had.

Nigel Gee had to work hard for the first time that day as he scanned the crowds to spot his man. 'There, sir,' he said, pointing. 'Man in the leather jacket, girl with the red trainers.'

Hester was all eyes for Leila. She was giggling with her male companion, dressed in black leggings that stopped just below the knees, a flimsy cream top, with silver jewellery dangling loose down her front – very hippyish. He hadn't requested any photographs to be taken of the people being chosen, but in Leila's case he wished now that he had. 'Quite charming,' he said to Nigel Gee, who nodded in agreement. They all watched Leila go in to see her movie, then they were off again. 'One more,' boomed Hester, like a general boosting the morale of his troops.

First they went to Hester's private club in Piccadilly for a couple of hours, where they had a well deserved drink and some wonderful food, and Frankie King was free to go out onto the roof terrace to smoke with all the other nicotine criminals.

Hester thanked Nigel Gee for all the good work. The day had been a self-indulgent exercise, and he could only really visualise Leila's face out of the four people he had seen, but he was another day closer. He checked his watch. 'Shall we go and finish off?'

They found Frankie King and headed to the car for their final destination of the day. As they entered a lap dancing establishment in Soho, Hester slapped Frankie King on the back and joked, 'I would have thought you'd have been a member here, Frankie, my son.' Frankie King laughed along with them. 'Get the drinks in, Frankie.'

No wonder he was a billionaire, thought Frankie King, still feeling the pain of the speeding ticket.

They propped up the bar. Nigel Gee was not in any rush to complete the business at hand, as he took in the entertainment on offer. He was particularly fascinated by a blonde lady with extremely long legs who was wearing sparkling golden high heel shoes - he was definitely a leg man.

'Is she on tonight?' asked Hester.

Nigel Gee looked at him as if having just being accused of

gross negligence. He raised a pointed finger to Hester's left. Hester turned, looked, continued with his drinking, and slowly took in the delicious movements of the scantily-dressed Cozzie, working her pole deliciously.

FOUR

Leila had been instructed to write a letter to her brother, telling him what she was taking part in and who he could contact, by email (definitely not in person), before becoming, as far as her foster parents were concerned, a missing person. She had enjoyed her week in London, staying with her new friend at his nice flat in Harringay, even when his girlfriend came home early from a dental conference and found her there, coming out of the shower. The poor woman had gone apoplectic with rage.

Now she was being dropped off in the Aston Martin at some hotel on the edge of London. In her new trainers, she skipped around the bonnet of the car to give him a big hug. It was really quite emotional – she didn't want to go. He made sure she had her hand luggage, told her she looked great and that everything would be fine. She told him she was sad to leave him. With a kiss on the cheek and a wave, she reluctantly went towards the woman who stood waiting for her in the entrance.

In Collyhurst, a grim suburb of Manchester, Henry was in the builders' yard tip that passed for the back garden of his terraced house, kissing his wife while his two young sons tried to hang onto their daddy's legs. Henry's wife was crying and reluctant to let him go.

'Come on, Tracy,' he said. 'You know this is a once in a lifetime deal.'

'I know, Henry. It's just so hard. And the boys.'

'Keep them busy with school and their football teams and they'll never know I've been away. Come on, girl, stop crying.'

While she tried to compose herself, Henry squatted down to the two boys. 'I'm going off on that big building job now, lads. You be good for your mum.' The one who looked more of a junior than an infant nodded firmly. 'You're my two top men.'

He kissed his sons' heads, kissed his wife fiercely on the lips, then went through his kitchen, picked up his holdall and let himself out the front door, without looking back. A sleek Mercedes sat waiting for him. He got into the back seat and closed the door.

The driver looked over his shoulder at him. 'No-one to wave you off, sir?'

'No, mate. I'm single at the moment. Very single.'

Claudia, due to financial restraints, had been living back at her parents' house in the northern outskirts of York for the last six months. Two days before she was due to leave for London she finally broke the news to them, and to her current, very casual boyfriend, Ben, in the living room. She thought her mother was having a stroke at the reaction she took, falling dramatically into a chair. She had always been such a cool mum, letting her go skiing with the school or clubbing with her friends at only seventeen, and not interfering with some of her idiot boyfriends, but there she was acting as if Claudia was being sent down for murder.

It was a good thing she had worked her notice at her job because there was no sleep to be had. Ben kissed her good night and went home to digest the news. Her mother continued ranting, telling her she would be horribly murdered, that it was the most sinister thing she had ever heard in her life. How could her daughter be so stupid and cruel to her own mother?

By the time the chauffeured car pulled up outside the house, her mother had subsided back to just being extremely unhappy and telling her to be careful with whoever she met and to watch what she ate.

Boyfriend, Ben, didn't bother to show up for the farewells.

In Clapham, while the driver waited by his Audi car, Will had to be tracked down by his uncle. Interfering, moronic, mates had to be threatened to fuck off, and then Will was bundled into the car, his luggage thrown in after him, the door slammed shut and the roof banged hard twice.

On the journey down from Liverpool, in the back of a chauffeur-driven Jaguar, Lee had maintained a simmering excitement, although he was interested to note that there had been no great wrench to leave Rachel. Maybe that would hit him later, if at all. He tried not to think too hard about what lay ahead of him. What would happen, would happen. The driver never said a word to him, even as they stopped at a service station, which amused Lee. He used the facilities, then sat outside with a sandwich and a soft drink, within sight of the car, and mentally tried to prepare himself for the time away. His real father had been into all that meditation stuff, one of the reasons he had been shown to be unliveable with. Lee shook his head to clear out the memories and walked to the Jaguar – let's get on with it, he thought.

Soon he was seeing signs for London. Once off the motorway, it wasn't long before they arrived outside an imposing hotel. He didn't bother to say thank you to his driver, just climbed out and went to the woman in the foyer who was waving at him. He was guided down the hotel corridor and into a conference room, the kind he had set up hundreds of times when working in Chester. Immediately, one thing grabbed his attention: a scale model of a two-storey building, with three wings that came together at a domed tower, and atop the tower a huge wind turbine. It was a well-made model, with even a few little cars on the car-park, realistic-looking trees and a fence around the perimeter.

Then a big bull of a man stood up, smiled and offered a handshake. 'I'm Michael. Michael Hester.'

'I'm Lee. You first here?'

'Apparently so. There's refreshments over there.'

'Oh, good.' He indicated the model. 'What the hell's this?'

'I've been puzzling over that myself. It must be where they're putting us.'

As Lee perused the buffet, they were joined by Henry,

who looked to be still dressed for the building site in dusty jeans and checked shirt. At least his footwear was civil enough. He said hello before going straight at the sandwiches. Then there was a flurry of arrivals with *Big Brother-style* introductions (where nobody remembered anyone's name). The couple from the York restaurant, Beverley and Tony, held hands as if someone was going to violently separate them. Young Will from Clapham took a plate of food and found a seat near the windows. Leila also kept herself to herself. Cozzie and Claudia, as the two most attractive girls, levitated towards each other and sat talking.

Henry returned to Lee's side, and asked, 'Where did they pick you up?'

'In Liverpool. You?'

'I was on a job in York. I'm from Manchester. Is this it, then? What have we got? Five women. Not bad odds.'

'One's married.'

'That never bothered me before.'

Cozzie said to Claudia, 'Six months locked away. I don't know whether I can handle it. There'd better be some booze. I can't go six months without a drink.'

'I can't go six months without sex, so one of these blokes...'

They collapsed into each other laughing.

Lee decided to assess the people he would be spending six months with, starting with the two giggly women. Even if they turned out to be two completely unfriendly bitches they would make nice eye candy, at least. The white girl had on very low-slung hipster jeans. The thing he noticed about the black girl, apart from her gorgeous teeth, were her leather boots with serious heels to them. The married couple seemed to be normal enough – the woman not overly attractive but with a cute bobbed haircut. He found another attractive woman talking with a Mexican-looking man with a very white smile. He was unsure about these two, for some reason. The middle-aged Asian man was staring out of the window, perhaps having second thoughts about what he was getting involved in. Near him was a sullen young man, engrossed in his food, who might prove to be a problem. The big, older man who he met first came across as trying too hard to look casual, as if he was hiding his desire to win – not that there was a prize on offer, as far as he knew. Henry, beside him, was easy enough, in his early thirties but with his mind still residing in his early twenties. He might become a little tedious if he wanted to become mates. The eastern European man was eating like there was no tomorrow. He might become troublesome if cabin fever set in. He almost failed to notice the lovely girl behind all the mingling bodies. What a sweetheart. But surely it was cruel to include such a young girl. Probably the women would take her into their group.

Lee drifted away from Henry to pour himself a glass of lemonade. He looked over the model again. It was definitely a shopping centre. He didn't know what he'd expected on the ride down – a big house, a farm complex, but not a shopping centre. Someone was calling for attention. Lee turned to see two suited men, with the doors being closed behind them. Like everyone else, he took a seat. Here we go, he thought, rules of the house. He looked to his left: the nervous Asian man. To his right: the quiet, young girl, blatantly staring at him.

'Hi,' he said to her. She didn't answer.

'Ladies and Gentlemen,' called one of the suits. 'Welcome to you all. My name is Frankie King, and this is Nigel Gee. We're here to finally tell you what this is all about. To answer all your questions, hopefully.' While he was talking, Nigel was going from person to person handing out envelopes. 'These contain five hundred pounds, for your inconvenience and expenses so far. This is extra to the main fee agreed upon.'

Lee smiled at seeing all the different reactions to an envelope stuffed with cash. The Asian man, Henry and the young man looked in straight away, while the girl next to him put it on her lap. There was a whoop from the black girl.

'Zombies!' shouted Frankie.

'Where?' asked Henry, deadpan, prompting laughter.

'Imagine, if you can, the end of the world. A plague! A meteor strike! A virus! You're running for your lives with only the few things you could grab hold of.'

Lee smiled again. He liked this guy.

'You end up,' continued Frankie, 'with a small group of fellow survivors, at a shopping mall. Zombies are banging on the windows, trying to get in and eat your flesh. You're trapped in there. What do you do? You get on with it, that's what you do. You make the best of it. That's what we're saying here. Eight o'clock tonight you'll be taken by executive bus to a sealed, completely real shopping mall, fully stocked like the one you went into last week, or last month. Once you're inside, you'll live there for exactly six months. It's completely up to you how you deal with it. You can go clothes shopping for free every day, you can eat in any of the many food outlets, play in any of the sports shops. Basically, it's all yours. Of course, by eight o'clock tonight if you decide this is not for you, then feel free to take your five hundred pounds and leave us. Once you're on the bus, you'll be given proof of the first instalment in your fee, so you're committed to it after that.'

Nobody was laughing any more. Everyone was looking at everyone else. Tony from Yorkshire stood up to ask a question, 'Are we to be filmed? Is that what it's about?'

'You will not be filmed in any way, whatsoever. There are security CCTV cameras in place, because it will be a real shopping centre next year, but feel free to smash them all if you wish.'

'Can I interject here?' asked Nigel Gee. 'Yes, it's your home, to do as you please, but remember you're still under the rule of English law, so if you get really bored and try to burn the building down, you will be charged with arson.'

'Thank you, Nigel. Nigel's a lawyer, by the way, everyone. Any more questions?'

Claudia wasn't shy. 'We're to be locked in together. No offence, but what if one of these men is a... you know... sexual...'

'Claudia, isn't it? Claudia, that could happen walking your doggy, could it not? As in life, while you're in there you make arrangements and build relationships to protect yourself from unpleasantness.'

'What if it gets really heavy? Would the police come in?'

'There will be no way to contact the police.'

Cathy asked, and they all noted her American accent for

the first time, 'Excuse me, what if one of us gets sick?'

'We have Dr Afridi here for that. If, for example, one of you needed to have an appendix removed, or there was a fall resulting in, say, a fractured skull, Dr Afridi alone will know the way to summon emergency assistance.'

To Lee, Dr Afridi looked none the wiser. Lee felt this was getting amazing, it was raising his blood pressure. He looked at the girl next to him. 'Hi,' he said again. 'I'm Lee.'

'I'm Leila.'

'Are you okay with this, Leila?'

'I suppose so. It's a bit scary, though.'

'Stick with me, kid. Where are you from, anyway?'

'London,' she lied.

'Oh, a local girl.'

'No more questions?' asked Frankie. 'Well, we'll be around all afternoon if you think of anything. Nigel has the contracts for you to look over. What is it they say about dinner parties? Seven thirty for eight? Be back in this room by seven thirty, please. With your forms signed. That is, unless you've decided not to stay with us.'

Some people went out of the room immediately, including Cozzie and Claudia. Cathy and Madesio stood talking with Beverley and Tony. Dr Afridi went back to his window. Lee wondered whether the doctor would hurt himself jumping from the second floor. He decided to take a walk himself. There was nothing to think about, he was going on the trip no matter what, but there was no rush to make friends, it wasn't the first day of school or anything – he laughed quietly to himself; the first day of senior school had started with him having to fight Dale Vernon, because

Dale wanted to be cock of the year and thought Lee looked really hard.

Down the corridor, seeking a way out, Lee realised he had Leila in tow. She had taken him literally at his word.

'Come on, Leila. At the moment I want to find out exactly where I am.'

They wandered through reception and out onto a suburban area beyond the hotel boundaries. They were certainly not in Central London. Leila decided to sit down on a low wall and seek out a mint from her handbag. Lee went further on to look at a road traffic sign.

'Why not just ask a receptionist?' pointed out Leila.

'Not just a pretty face, are you? It said Wembley, that way. North London, then.'

'Do you want a mint?'

'Thank you.' He sat beside her and took the proffered sweet. 'Is Wembley anywhere near you?'

'No.'

'So, Leila, are you definitely going for this? How old are you, by the way? What do your parents say?'

Leila crinkled her brow at fielding the age question again. She considered herself more streetwise than some of the people she had just seen in the hotel suite. 'I'm sixteen. My mum's in Styal prison.'

That didn't quite answer his questions. It puzzled him, though, because he knew Styal was in Cheshire. He let it go, anyway.

FIVE

Cathy and Madesio had come over from New York on the same American Airlines flight without knowing it. Since meeting in the foyer of the London hotel they had stuck close together, mainly due to their shared nationality, though they did immediately like each other anyway. They talked of family left behind, and the fact that he mentioned his family being massive, yet didn't bore her with it, endeared him to her. They agreed that they both felt like they were living in a dream since the whole thing began. It was frightening, but would surely be a great adventure. As for Cathy, who liked all things British, just to be on English soil for the first time gave her a thrill. She talked Madesio into finding a shop with her later on, just to get some silly souvenir. After six months confinement they might just want to run to the airport. He said he was happy to go along with her.

Cozzie and Claudia went to the Ladies together, then found the hotel bar, where they were joined by Henry and Alexandru, although the Romanian hardly said a word. Both men were already being assessed as potential mates for the experiment. Claudia looked at Cozzie, trying to express her thoughts that what they had here were two good-looking guys but with personalities a little lacking. She remembered Henry from their brief meeting in the York pub. Nevertheless, they all had a drink and a laugh together, taking their minds off the stressful day.

Cathy and Madesio found the others, minus Will, in the inner, cobbled courtyard of the hotel, some drinking tea or coffee. The pros and cons were being discussed. Could they face what was ahead? Would they go out of their minds? Was it worth it? For Beverley and Tony it certainly was, although they didn't say as much. Their B&B hotel in Malton, North Yorkshire was doing very badly; so, even in high season, they had cancelled their few guests and locked the place up. Come out somewhere around Christmas with £200,000 and start again, that was the plan.

Dr Afridi spoke for the first time when Beverley expressed surprise that he could find the time for such a thing. 'I'm between placements at the moment. I'll call this a mini-sabbatical.'

'Good to have a doctor on board,' said Tony.

Dr Afridi smiled at him.

'Can we possibly all get along?' asked Cathy. 'A couple of those other guys don't seem too friendly.'

'I think we'll be fine,' said Tony. 'If the group stays together, the individuals can't be that disruptive.'

Beverley seemed quite proud of her husband's little speech. She turned to Cathy and Madesio and told them about her relative in Florida.

'It's a great state,' said Cathy. 'I have cousins in the Keys.'

'Oh, I don't think my own cousin is that far down. Near

Orlando, I believe. We'll be going to visit after all this.'

'Then you must come to stay in Buffalo.'

'Goodness, that *is* in the north. Near Niagara Falls, am I right?'

'Sure. We'll take you there.'

'Push her over, in a barrel,' joked Tony.

Will made an appearance, drinking from a coke bottle. Tony decided to go over and speak to him – there was no point having someone feel left out. They all watched the encounter. Tony came back nodding. 'Seems like a nice lad. He's a bit nervous. He'll be fine.'

'Oh, good,' said Beverley. 'Should we go and find the others?'

'Perhaps we should give them a little time,' suggested Dr Afridi. 'Everyone has their own way of getting used to this thing.'

Killing some time themselves, Lee and Leila asked a passer-by for directions to any nearby shops and were pointed towards a petrol station around the bend in the road. They strolled off in that direction and, as they approached, could see cars waiting to buy fuel, getting backed up into a long queue.

'More rumours about a strike, no doubt,' said Lee, shaking his head. 'Morons.'

Two police cars sped by with their blue lights and sirens going, heading to a separate incident.

The two of them stood outside the shop, discussing what they could possibly buy that wouldn't be in their new home. Undecided, he bought ten packets of his favourite chewy sweets, a torch and a cigarette lighter, for no particular reason. She got some batteries for her iPod and bought them both an ice lolly for the walk back.

A little late afternoon sun flooded over them on the way back down the road and it was very pleasant out there. For a moment he imagined he was sixteen again, on school holidays back home with his first girlfriend. That had been Joanna, a mouthy blonde, who was the complete opposite of this delicate, mysterious brunette. He slurped his lolly to make her smile at him, and it was a lovely smile indeed, incorporating the eyes as well.

'Have you got a girlfriend?' Leila asked him, by coincidence.

'That's a hard question to answer, Leila. I have and I haven't, because of going away like this for six months.'

'It's tough, yeah. I understand.'

'What about you?'

'I had a couple recently in B... back home. They just wanted sex all the time. I don't need it in my life right now.'

Her candid comment threw him for a moment. 'Yeah, that's the right attitude.'

She suddenly stopped dead. 'Lee, I'm starting to get frightened.'

'Hey.' He found it a natural thing to hold her. He almost told her to forget the whole thing and get herself off home. 'Everything will be cool. Once you settle in, you'll rule the place. Trust me.'

'The money will be good to have, won't it?'

'Of course it will.'

'For when my mum gets out.'

'That's right, keeping thinking that way.' He would have liked to hold her for a while longer, but his lolly was melting down his hand. He bent her over in a mock attempt to lick his fingers and she giggled brightly. 'Come on, let's get back. We can make some new friends.'

After they had all gathered back in the hotel conference suite, Frankie King did at least tell them they would be going somewhere in Berkshire, as perhaps a small saver in case they went stir crazy. Nigel Gee made sure he collected all their signed release forms. Cozzie was slightly tipsy after five hours in the bar. She took Frankie aside and asked him, 'There will be some alcohol in this gaff we're going to?'

He played along, remembering her from the lap-dancing club. 'A little. Find it and hide it.'

'I'll do that.'

There was another little buffet set out for them. Catering worker Lee thought the hotel had put on a good show for them. He'd definitely come again.

They left just after eight o'clock in the evening, in a very posh executive coach. Lee pretended he was a Manchester City football player going to an away match. Everyone spread out along the seating. Will felt like a nap, so took the whole of the back seat to himself. Two hotel porters, perhaps having gotten whiff of what they were up to, were there to wave them off. And then at the main entranceway they were cheered away by what could only be described as a female crew of Romanian pickpockets, in full traditional garb. 'Hey!' cried Henry. 'They must be Alex's relatives! Hiya! Alex, look.' But he realised Alexandru was not on the coach. 'What the hell?'

'Looks like he decided not to go,' said Hester, sitting just in front.

SIX

Leila sat beside Lee, of course. He was happy to have her with him; there was no nuisance value at all with the girl. They shared his chewy sweets and had an earpiece each of her iPod. He made her laugh whenever he complained about her choice of music. There was Leona Lewis, Darren Hayes, Coldplay, The Saturdays. He feigned a heart attack and cried, 'Oh, my God!' when One Direction came on.

At one point in the journey, Claudia, sitting inside Cozzie, leant across the aisle and said, 'You two have become close very quickly.' Lee just nodded at her. He sensed Leila tense up, and had the impression that if the younger girl had not been up against the window then Claudia might have gotten a smack in the mouth.

Realising she might have sounded like a cow, Claudia offered her packet of liquorice allsorts. 'Want one? What have you got there?' They exchanged sweets all round and the moment passed.

The weather had deteriorated, so the summer night went dark on the motorway very quickly. Lights came on along the seats, the readers in the group being Beverley and Cathy.

Back in the hotel they had compared their thick volumes of Stephen King and Colleen McCullough, and laughed at the thought of one of them having a WH Smith all to herself and the other a Waterstones.

Most of the men were asleep. Only Madesio, used to long, unsociable hours with his work, sat wide awake. He was watching Frankie King and Nigel Gee in the front seats. The two organisers were checking their boots and waterproof coats and hats, seemingly getting ready for the delivery stage of their mission. Madesio guessed they were to be dumped in a cold, possibly dark, cavern of a shopping mall and made to endure an unpleasant first night.

He wasn't wrong. For the last twenty minutes of the journey the rain had lashed the coach windows. They passed through the orange glow of a small town, without even a dog out on the streets, before it was pitch dark and they were slowing to find an entrance in a gigantic fence, Frankie King standing to advise the driver. Suddenly there were fireworks going off everywhere, mimicking explosions, it felt to Madesio, waking all the sleepers and scaring Cozzie, in particular.

The coach moved slowly through the darkness, then came to a stop. Everyone who cared to look could make out the white lines of parking spaces on the tarmac. A huge building loomed in the near distance, indeed not very well lit.

'Let's go, people!' cried Frankie King. 'The sooner you start, the sooner you finish! Off you get. It's thataway!'

Police sirens were blared at them as they filed down off the bus, into the torrential rain. Beverley and Cathy cried out in their confused discomfort. It was Tony who took command. 'Stick together!' he shouted over the noise of firework bombs, the sirens and the weather. 'Follow me, everyone!'

Lee grabbed Leila's hand. They were last off the bus, apart from Will. Lee looked back to make sure he was with them and saw the boy smiling for the first time. So, he liked the action, did he?

'Come on, Leila, run,' said Lee.

They caught the others and were relieved to get under cover, in an entranceway with the thousand shopping trolleys. The doors were open to a foyer lit by emergency lighting. There was a fountain, switched off, toilets, wooden benches around a garden feature, a sloping map table of the mall and a couple of red post boxes. Everyone watched Tony go inside, as if waiting to see if a large net would fall down on top of him.

'Come on,' said Beverley. 'We'll catch our deaths out here. Let's get in and get dry.'

Will was last over the threshold, turning to watch the two automatic doors slide shut, for the next six months.

Naturally, a little disorientated and unhappy, they all stayed where they were in the foyer. Henry and Dr Afridi did drift inside a little way just to look off into the gloomy marble concourse of one of the wings. Madesio and Claudia went in search of towels in the immediate vicinity but came back empty handed.

'We have to get to the nearest shop,' said Beverley.

There was no great rush to move.

'A couple of us can go,' said Lee, bringing out his torch sooner than he expected to use it. 'We'll bring stuff out. We might find the light switch, as well.'

Henry and Madesio volunteered to go with him, and they started to laugh once they were off down the silent hallway – what were they all getting in a state about?

'Are we going to find zombies?' joked Madesio.

Familiar smaller stores were on the periphery of the mall. Lee recognised a Homeware store. 'That'll do. But shall we see what's at the end of here first?'

They continued on, and came out into a massive atrium, gloomy and ghostly as it was, but still impressive – a coffee chain had the centre food court area of the floor, with above it hanging a huge Superman-style crystal configuration which would no doubt be stunning in daylight. Around the vast circular hall they recognised major stores such as Next and Disney, and a cinema, and a selection of food outlets. A two-storey McDonald's restaurant started the way off into another wing – Lee would investigate that in his own good time.

'Let's get some Next clothes,' said Lee. 'Start as we mean to go on. Then we get towels on the way back.'

'Why not bring everyone down here?' asked Henry. 'There's nothing to be frightened of.'

'Everyone's a little spooked at the moment,' pointed out Madesio.

So they went with Lee's plan, collecting trousers and tops from the darkened Next store and putting them in Next carrier bags. It was a novel experience, to say the least.

'What about the lighting?' asked Henry.

'We'll have to get through tonight, I suppose,' answered Lee. 'What about places to sleep?' He stepped over a low fence into the coffee shop's seating area and looked up and around him. 'Two different bedding places up there. Plus the one we're getting towels from.'

They went back to the others, picking up a dozen large towels on the way. Lee got a hug from Leila, as if he had survived a dangerous mission. At this rate, he thought, they'd be married by the time they got out.

The Ladies and Gents were used to towel down and change clothes. Then the best dressed refugees in the world gathered to assess the state of play. The initial shock had gone. Beverley and Cathy accepted that they probably weren't going to get any proper lighting, so they were keen to bed down for the night.

'Shall all the girls go in one bed store and the guys in the other?' suggested Cathy. 'Of course, Beverley and Tony, you can find your own place, if you'd prefer.'

'I'm hungry,' stated Cozzie, not quite in full petulant model mode.

A few of the others said the same. Madesio volunteered again to provide food, which could be consumed where they were, and then they could all move in as a group when it was time to sleep. Claudia wanted to go with Madesio – her feistiness had returned. Suddenly from back where the three men had just come from, there came loud smashing noises. The females were instantly upset by it. Lee looked at Henry, and they silently agreed to investigate. Hester patted Lee on the back and went along with them.

They walked towards the clanging and smashing of glass.

The noise became quite loud in the dead of night. Henry's shadowy face looked a bit nervous, in Lee's opinion. They were both glad to have the bulky Hester there. They easily identified a fried chicken outlet as the source of the racket. The front window had been put in. As they stepped inside, they could see most of the advertising logos had been shattered and tables and chairs were upended. Then they saw Will amidst all the chaos. He looked feral and extremely agitated, but when he spoke to them he seemed cheery and upbeat.

'These fuckers gave me the sack last month!'

SEVEN

All the men spent the night in the downstairs Homeware shop, from where they got the towels, while the women were upstairs in Bedlington's bed store, next to McDonald's, once it had been checked for bogeymen. Beverley and Tony agreed to be separated just for the first night, to prove they were team players.

Lee woke in his own double bed with red satin sheets. Firstly, he reached for Rachel before remembering where he was. After excavating his eyes, he propped himself up and looked about him. Dr Afridi, Madesio and Tony were still asleep, but Hester and Henry were sitting up in their beds. Will was in the process of getting dressed. Lee was reminded of his drug trial in the Manchester clinic.

As Will went to leave, Henry called after him, 'Hey, Will. Have you worked in a lot of places?'

Henry and Hester laughed. Will grinned at them as he went out.

Lee was one of those people who couldn't stay in bed once he was awake. He jumped up and dressed in his new Next jeans and sweater. He stood into his old trainers - they would have to be replaced. 'Morning, gents,' he said to the two in bed.

'What are you having for breakfast?' asked Henry. 'Chinese, Indian or Thai?'

'I'll go and see what I fancy.'

First of all he walked to the place they had made their entrance the night before, wanting to look outside. But all he could see was several hundred yards of car-park terminating at a high grey-metal wall, topped with razor wire. Feeling hungry, he went to the central area. There was a plethora of palm trees and gold columns. As expected, the crystal sculpture which went high to the dome roof, was extremely impressive. He spotted Beverley and Cathy entering an Italian diner, but he chose to scavenge in a sandwich bar. He made a sandwich with fresh ingredients and opened a carton of milk.

Back out front, he met Claudia, looking tired and with her hair up in a ponytail. The Next clothes she had ended up with were a bit gaudy and oversized. It was so obvious what he was thinking that she made a little pose for him.

'What do you think?' she asked for his playful opinion.

'All the rage this summer. Have you eaten?'

'I've had some tea and toast. I was going to have a wander about. Want to come along?'

'Sure. We can be the pioneers.'

They walked up a shut-down escalator, went past the store where the girls slept, moving along above the wing they came in through. All the shops were household names but they felt no urge to go looting. At the far end, they found lifts that wouldn't open when the buttons were pressed. The view through the panoramic window was similar to Lee's initial one – uninspiring.

They turned back and came along the other side, occasionally looking to the level below. Lee examined the high glass roof curving above them, which reminded him of a Victorian railway station. One thing was sure, it would never be gloomy in there during the day. They just had to make sure there was lighting in the evenings.

'This is all pretty normal,' she said.

'Maybe it gets more exciting in the other parts.'

'Did you sleep well?'

'Yes, I always sleep best with a group of strange men.'

'That should be my line. So, never been in the army, then?'

'Do I not look like I've been in the army?'

'You're too small.'

'Yeah, but I'm surprisingly hard.'

'Are you, indeed?'

They watched Cozzie leave the bed store in a sarong and noisy flip-flops, heading off to find breakfast.

They moved off down a second walkway, the one dominated by a McDonald's. It made him think about work, and Rachel and about Will's late-night vandalism. 'What did you think of Will smashing that place up?'

'I thought it was a bit odd. I hope he doesn't get out of hand.' She stopped, made a grasp for his forearm. 'Oh, this is more like it. Miss Selfridge here, Gap there. River Island up ahead. Do I sound shallow to you?'

'Not at all. But you should pace yourself.'

'I suppose you're right. I might overdose on shopping.

Still, I've got to get out of these things. Can we pop in Debenhams?'

'Yeah, I find I have the time.'

Normally, with Rachel especially, Lee would not be able to stand accompanying a girl out shopping. Under the current circumstances he found it actually interesting, even giving his opinion of things she expressed an interest in. She settled on a blouse and faded jeans.

'This feels so wrong,' she said, unclipping the clothes from the hangers.

He realised she intended to change right there and then. 'Do you want me to turn around?'

She laughed. 'If you want. I'm not fussed.'

The Next top came off. There wasn't an ounce of fat on her, her stomach completely smooth. Average sized boobs in a white bra, although he did try not to look. The yellow Next leggings came off.

'Different coloured knickers,' she said. 'It's a Yorkshire thing.'

'Yorkshire? I had you down as a Geordie.'

'No, you didn't.'

She took another brief deliberate examination of the blouse's label before putting it on. Good God, he thought, that was a bit naughty. He couldn't handle six months of that kind of teasing. She got into the jeans and he watched the buttoning up slowly above that erotic midriff.

'Shall we move on?' she said.

They left Debenhams and continued along. WH Smith came up on the right, then a Carphone Warehouse.

'Did they tell you not to try to use your mobile?' she

asked.

'Yes, they did. They've blocked the signal, so no point, really.'

'I might upgrade mine before we leave. Are you not changing your clothes?'

He laughed, not expecting that. By the time he'd considered undressing in front of her, they had reached the end. A large Jon Lewis store dominated here. No doubt Marks & Spencer would block off the third wing.

There were more lifts, and also a fire exit set into an alcove, with a large window. The view was much improved – woodland, a distant hill farm and one property within shouting distance of the fence. Lee wondered whether the occupants knew what was going on in the shopping mall. They decided against taking the fire exit stairs, there was still a spooky novelty to the place, so went back along the opposite side. Downstairs, they saw Hester and Dr Afridi taking their own initial tour of the building.

'Dr Afridi doesn't seem quite with it,' she said.

'He's probably a morphine addict. Hey, there's a sports shop. You can help me choose some new trainers.'

It was then that she screamed.

Lee jumped out of his skin, grabbed for her as she threw herself into his shoulder, looking for what had suddenly shocked her. On the marble floor a short distance ahead of them sat a red mass, on top of a wide pool of blackened blood. It was a combination of shredded torso and splattered entrails. She peeked another look and had to hold on to her tea and toast.

'Jesus Christ,' muttered Lee.

The scream had made Hester and Dr Afridi run up the nearest escalator and join them. Lee indicated the cadaver. Hester and the doctor went forward, Hester looking back, calling, 'Take her away, Lee.'

He followed the instruction, guiding Claudia downstairs. Cathy and Beverley were within hailing distance, doing a little window shopping. They hurried over and took charge of Claudia.

'There seems to be a body up there,' answered Lee to Beverley's accusing look.

Lee watched them go. This was getting heavy, he thought. He considered returning up the escalator, until he noticed the blood that had dripped to ground level, so instead followed the three women back at a distance.

The group all gathered at news of the grim discovery. It was the first time Leila had seen Lee that morning, and the terrible business gave her the excuse to hug him once again.

'Are you all right?' she asked.

'I'm fine, Leila. Bit of a shock, that's all.'

Will, who had commandeered a mountain bike to get around, set off to see the corpse for himself. Claudia was made to sit down and offered tea or a glass of water.

'Should we get the doctor?' asked Cozzie.

Claudia assured them that she was fine. She smiled at Lee, something that put Leila's petite nose out of joint. The younger girl went back to her breakfast of English muffin and coffee. She had wanted a McDonald's milkshake but hadn't known if the machine was on, or in fact safe to use. She wished the oldies would get on with solving the little problems of the place.

Lee got himself a simple coffee from the main shop. When he came out, Hester and Dr Afridi were approaching the group. Will overtook them on his bike and did an annoying semi-wheelie stop on the front wheel.

'It's all right!' called Hester.

'What is it?' asked Beverley.

'Dr Afridi is sure it's not human. Aren't you, doctor?'

'Oh, yes, most certainly. It's a deer, or some such creature.'

'How did it get in here?' asked Henry.

'It's a plant, obviously,' said Hester.

'I thought the doctor said it was a deer?' joked Henry.

Hester grinned. 'It's part of the game, anyway. Make us think it's a zombie kill.'

'Oh, that's very good,' said Tony.

'Is it staying there?' asked Cozzie, pulling a face.

'No, no,' answered Hester. 'It's got to be gotten rid of.'

'But how?' asked Cathy. 'We're locked in, are we not?'

'From the roof,' said Lee. 'Over the side. We've got to check the fire exits, anyway. There must be a way up there. So, we'll get it up and throw it off.'

'I'm with you, mate,' said Henry.

'Okay.' Lee turned to Leila. 'Coming along? We'll wrap it before you get close.'

Leila smiled up at him. 'I'm good here, thanks.'

Lee and Henry went via a DIY shop, to pick up rubber gloves and a wheelbarrow, and a Hessian sack to cover it with.

As he assessed the dead animal, Lee said, 'We'll have to come back and clean up the area.'

'Disinfect it, yeah. Come on, you take the nice end.'

They loaded the wheelbarrow, threw the sack over the creature and headed to the stairwell near Jon Lewis. Once through the fire door there was a spiral walkway as well as stairs, so they didn't have to carry the wheelbarrow up. At the top, Henry kicked open the door and they lifted the barrow out onto white gravel. They took the chance first to take a panoramic look around. The thing that dominated everything was the gigantic wind turbine above the central dome, currently not moving.

'I bet the neighbours love that,' said Henry, sarcastically.

'You don't think we have to get it moving so we can have lights at night?'

Henry pulled a look of disbelief at Lee.

Mostly it was countryside all around them, they were certainly out in rural Berkshire, if they were in Berkshire, but then as they crossed to the other side of the roof, weaving between square air-conditioning units, they could make out the tops of houses of a small town.

'They're all dead over there,' kidded Henry.

'Come on, let's get rid of that thing.'

They carried the wheelbarrow to an edge.

'The whole thing?' asked Henry.

'Why not?'

They threw both dead animal and wheelbarrow as far off as they could. They were just turning to head back in, when both of them realised they had spotted something. After looking at each other, they turned their gaze down to the car park.

EIGHT

Everyone stood on the roof above Jon Lewis. They looked down, awestruck at the sight that faced them.

'How's that done?' asked Cathy.

'Not a clue,' answered Claudia.

'Animatronics, maybe,' suggested Madesio.

'Now, that's completely bizarre,' said Beverley.

Moving very slowly across the car park were dozens of robotic zombies, wearing torn and blood-stained clothing, their movements all exactly the same, and even at that distance the facial features, though an attempt had been made to make them look ravaged, were pretty vague. It was the oddest thing any of them had ever seen.

'Sorry, remind me,' said Tony. 'Are we not being filmed? Because somebody has gone to great lengths here.'

'I thought that even before the zombies, darling,' said his wife.

'Extraordinary,' was Dr Afridi's comment. 'We shall have the fun of seeing those throughout our stay.'

'Not my idea of fun,' said Cozzie, turning away with a model's pout.

'Hey, people!' shouted Will.

Some of them had not heard the boy speak before, so looked at him with surprise. He was pointing at a blackboard that stood up against the side of the building.

They gathered round to read the message.

You will find information on how to deal with zombies in one of the post boxes. Only over-25's permitted to do this task.

'Who does that leave us with?' asked Cathy.

'Me,' said Madesio. 'Tony, Beverley.'

'You can leave me out, thank you' said Beverley, with a smile.

'Mr Hester?' continued Madesio.

'Everyone just calls me Hester. Please, Hester will be fine. I'm up for going. Tony, are you coming?'

'Sure. Any ladies want to join us?'

There were no female takers. Hester, Tony and Madesio tramped down and across to the original entranceway. Madesio manhandled one of the post boxes but it seemed to be a genuinely strong Royal Mail post box. Hester tried the second, and the door opened. After glancing at the others, he delved inside. He brought out a postcard, with a key attached by an elastic band.

'What does it say?' asked Tony.

Hester read the card. 'This key opens the other post box.'

Tony found that hilarious. Hester unlocked the other box. From it he lifted out a black metal rifle, followed by a box of ammunition. He stayed down on one knee, looking at his two comrades. 'Seriously, guys, a rifle? We are allowed to shoot zombies from the roof?'

Tony stopped laughing. He sat on a nearby bench. 'Good grief. Well, you know, that might be fun. But we really shouldn't have a rifle in here.'

'I agree,' said Madesio. 'That's off the scale, man.'

'Well,' said Hester. 'We either chuck it after the dead deer, or leave it locked in here. I could keep the key round my neck, if ever we feel like playing.'

'I'm happy for Hester to do that,' said Madesio.

'Okay,' said Tony. 'Shall we keep this between us three for now?'

'But what do we say to the others?' asked Madesio.

Hester stood up. 'Leave that to me. I'll tell them some gobbledegook. Something like there being air horns we can let off to have them moving one way and then the other. It'll be like a Benny Hill sketch out there, I'll say. They'll quickly forget the whole thing.'

They all nodded agreement, and Hester locked the rifle back up.

'Plenty of time for zombie shooting,' said Tony, as they headed back.

The great organiser, Beverley, called them all to the seats outside the coffee shop in the main atrium. Cozzie was the last to join the meeting, sulkily asking, 'What's all this about?' as she slumped down.

'It's a melting pot,' said Beverley, brightly. 'I thought we could toss ideas into the pot.'

'It's a toss pot,' said Lee, finding smirking appreciation from Claudia and Henry.

Beverley pressed on, regardless. 'I thought we'd better discuss things. Such as permanent sleeping arrangements and food management.'

'And the lights,' put in Cathy.

'And the lights. I thought we could allocate teams to make assessments of the key issues. Tony and I will check out the sleeping options. I'm sure we don't all want to stay in communal mode. Perhaps some of you could volunteer to inspect food supplies and food hygiene issues. We want to avoid getting poorly in here. And someone could try to figure out if we'll have electric light tonight.'

'I've got a background in catering,' said Lee. 'I'll go round and put together a report. Dr Afridi, maybe you'll come with me?'

Dr Afridi nodded his compliance.

'I'll look into the lighting,' said Hester.

It was the lull after the storm of arrival. Everyone was sitting around without much energy.

'I'm wondering about shower facilities,' continued Beverley. 'Anybody want to look into that.'

'We will,' answered Cathy, for both herself and Madesio.

'Thank you. Now, as to smoking.'

'Hang on,' interrupted Cozzie, the only one with a lit cigarette in her hand. 'If you add up the people here by the square yardage in this place, a couple of cigarettes on the go won't mean a bloody thing.'

'I was just going to say exactly that, Cozzie.'

'Oh! All right, then. I withdraw my strop.'

'I don't think anyone objects. I was just thinking of safety. You and the other smokers will take care, won't you?'

'Of course.'

'Well, apart from the things I've mentioned, I should think everything else will develop naturally – routine and entertainment. I've brought cards, if anybody would like to play some evening. No? Well, the offer's there.'

Lee had checked on Claudia's wellbeing while up on the roof. As he and Dr Afridi left to tour the food outlets, he paused near to her. 'Want to come and count frozen burgers?'

'I'll give that a miss, thank you. But, make sure to tell me all about it later.'

They shared a smile and he set out.

Not one to sit around, Henry went along with Hester to investigate the electrics. They found their way down into the bowels of the building via the corridor that held the crèche, a disabled toilet and the security suite. It was unnerving walking with only the security lighting to guide their way. They made small talk, such as where they were from and favourite football teams – Manchester City and Arsenal (if pushed to choose). They found dozens of cupboards and little rooms, a few times fearing they were getting themselves hopelessly lost, and, of course, it was all rough down there with unplastered walls and exposed pipe work.

'So, you're a builder, Henry?'

'Yes, seven years of that now.'

'Times are tough though, are they not? Is there much work out there?'

'True, it's been a nightmare. I've been all over the North West chasing work. This silliness in here should help me out, though.'

'Good, that's good. Maybe you could turn your hand to something else, when this is over? Diversify a bit. Maybe I could put you in touch with some people.'

'That could be great. You didn't say, what's your field?'

'Oh, fingers in many pies, my friend, fingers in many pies. Ah, look there, experience tells me it's always a good sign when it says "electrical cupboard."'

They spent ten minutes resolving the lighting issue, then continued on exploring even further beneath the mall. It was very musty down there. They came out of a staff fire door into what seemed like a large subway station, complete with tiled curving walls.

'What the fuck is this?' asked Henry. 'Do trains come through here?'

Hester stepped forward to examine the tracks. 'Trams, it looks like to me. It's a park and ride system. Shoppers park their car somewhere else and hop onto a tram to come into here.' He walked further along the track . There were wide walkways either side which went up to locked metal gates. 'Yeah, the people go up and down these, see.'

Henry indicated the dark tunnels either end of the cavernous area. 'I'm starting to imagine something nasty coming out of one of those tunnels. Let's get back.'

Hester laughed. 'Right you are, then.'

Dr Afridi armed himself with a pen and a clipboard, with a mini-plan of the building on the flipside. Lee made sure he had his torch and they set off on their food fact- finding mission. They started close to the centre, ignoring

McDonald's for the time being, because he knew how well that would be stocked, and skipped the smashed up premises of Will's former employer altogether. Slowly they compiled a list of what food was where, what was perishable and what was frozen. After a productive ninety minutes or so, and without even looking in Marks & Spencer, they were satisfied the group could survive for well over a year, so made their way back.

Dr Afridi spotted a Boots chemist, so they diverted across for him to take a brief medical inventory and to fill a carrier bag with utensils and basic first-aid items.

'I'm surprised you didn't bring your little black bag, Doc.'

'They wouldn't let me. That Frankie fellow said I lost it in the scramble to survive the first few hours.'

Lee smiled. 'He should be on the stage.'

'You said you're in catering, Lee. Does that mean you'll be doing some of the cooking?'

'You must be joking. If someone else wants to cook for everyone, that's fine, I'll supervise.'

Most of the group were still in the same place when they got back. Leila had gone walkabout.

'Unlimited supplies,' Lee told them. 'We could never eat it all.'

'Now that's such a waste, really,' said Cathy.

'I don't even think it's a case of even eating all the perishable goods first before we start on the cans and the frozen stuff. Basically, we can go mad. Dr Afridi thought, on the health side of things, we could have a list of outlets. Then after a couple of weeks we stop using them one by one, because I'm sure no-one wants to clean up or unblock the fryers. He suggests we have an initial rota for cleaning, a burst of action to take away the residue of the building work and the outfitting of the place. Then just basic hygiene to keep us healthy.'

'Excellent,' said Beverley. 'I'm good at rotas.'

'There's unlimited bottled water and soft drinks. Probably best not to try making milkshakes. I'm a McDonald's man, so I'll go in there this afternoon and check it out.'

'So, the freezers are on in the building?' asked Tony. 'That means the power's there for the lighting.'

'The lighting will be on,' called Hester, returning with Henry. 'We think we got to the bottom of it, didn't we Henry?'

'Yeah, we found a big switch and dropped it.'

NINE

Lee and Claudia decided to finish their interrupted walk round the mall.

'You've changed clothes again,' he noted.

'Yes, they were an impulse buy.' She looked down at her light summer dress, with practical leggings underneath and white trainers. 'What do you think?'

'Very nice. I'm disappointed I missed the changing, though.'

They came upon a different sports shop (staying away from the place where the dead animal had lain). It was a chance for Lee to change his own trainers. It was still gloomy inside the stores – Hester's miracle had not yet provided twenty-four hour lighting. They moved between the racks of sportswear, never something to get excited about even in normal times. Up a curved stairway they could see the footwear on the walls and also the gear for exclusive sports such as cricket and rugby. Once up there, Lee put in a few sharp blows to a punch bag.

'Ooh, you are quite hard, after all,' said Claudia.

'Shall we have a go at croquet?'

'I'll pass, thank you.'

They stood in front of the trainers.

Lee cocked his head, 'Over here.'

'That's the children's section.'

'I've got very small feet.'

She laughed. 'I suppose it's cheaper for you when you're in the real world.'

'I normally go for all black. But in here, shall I push the boat out?'

'Why not? Yellow Adidas. Bright red Nike.'

After a frenzy of trying-on, leaving the area littered with unwanted shoes, he settled on a brown pair of Rockport hiking boots.

'Yes, I know,' he said, looking down at his feet as they left. 'Not very fancy, but they feel great.'

'That's all that matters in a survival situation.'

'Yes, I agree, so get that sexy dress off. And put on a boiler suit.'

Back on the walkway they could tell it was raining on the high roof. He then finally saw what that particular section was called. 'Turbine Gallery. I think I see what they've done here. There are three arms stretching out from the middle. The place has been designed to look like a wind turbine. The walkways are the three blades.'

'It's a wind turbine lying flat on its back, which is the best thing that could happen to it.'

'Didn't go along with the revolution, I see?'

'The big con, you mean.'

'That way now? I suppose we'll call this the North Blade.'

'Is it north?'

'I don't know, I've not got a compass. I've got a cigarette lighter.'

'Eh?'

'Never mind.'

'Can we go in Beaverbrook's?'

'Whatever for?'

'Nice diamonds to wear while I'm playing at survival.'

Beaverbrook's the jewellers was firmly locked down. She made a sulky face and they moved on.

'Are you staying put in Bedlington's?' he asked.

'Why, do you want me to shack up with you?'

'There's an idea. So, what do you think of it so far?'

'I suppose I'm okay with it all. It's not Magaluf, but it beats working for a living.'

'What did you tell your family? Have you left a boyfriend pining for you out there?'

'No, no boyfriend. Well, there was this guy called Ben. Nothing serious. I told my parents everything. They called the police, the family solicitor, everyone, in fact, to try to get me to change my mind. Finally, they accepted that it was no different really to *I'm A Celebrity, Get Me Out Of Here*. It's just a reality show without the cameras.'

'They called the police?'

'Yeah, my mum's a bit melodramatic. She thought I was being swindled in some way.'

'This is like a reality show, as you say, but have you thought what the point of it all is?'

'Can't say I have, no.'

Cathy and Madesio, out and about counting showers and

making a note of their locations, explored down the same way Hester and Henry had gone, and found the General Manager's office, with its own bathroom. So, on their recommendation, Beverley and Tony set up home in there and became the first settled refugees.

Claudia did choose to stay in Bedlington's alongside Cozzie, Leila and Cathy. Most of the boys stayed where they were too, except Hester who dragged a bed into, of all places, an Ann Summers shop and made himself cosy amongst the lingerie. He told them he liked the feel of the carpet and the leather sofas in there. He used the nearby disabled facilities as his own personal shower room.

So, by the evening of day two, some kind of normality had started to develop. The lights came on at 1800 hrs. Lee pulled a shift in McDonald's and they all went in there for burgers and coke. It turned into a bit of a party.

Lee sat with his feet up, watching Leila nibble on a cheeseburger next to him. She and Cozzie had dressed up for the occasion – Leila in black top and black hot-pants taken from one of the younger, trendy stores, as well as black leggings with silver sparkly bits. Her hair was done in a way that suggested Cozzie had helped her with it.

'Are you all right?' he asked her.

'I'm good.'

He looked at Cathy, to his other side. 'Do you ever bother with McDonald's food? With all the choice you have in America?'

'Sometimes we do. This is very nice of you, thank you.'

Madesio gave him a smile and a thumbs up.

Lee watched everyone, all talking and integrating. Even

Will was there chatting to Hester. In Lee's opinion, this crazy thing could not have got off to a better start. He could have done without the dead animal, he supposed, but never mind.

He could hear Tony talking about turbines. So he had figured it out, as well – good man. Leila touched his hand. 'Yes, my darling?'

'What are we doing tonight?'

'Shall we go out somewhere?'

She giggled, crinkling her freckly nose.

'I was hoping to stay in,' she said, 'and play cards with Beverley.'

'You wild child, you. We could go on the roof and watch zombies walk about the car-park.'

Leila waited for Cathy and Madesio, who were moving off to join in a conversation with Hester. 'Lee, I don't really want to sleep in Bedley...whatever it's called.'

'You want your own place? Listen, stay in there tonight. In the morning we'll find you the perfect pad. I'll get a bed down to wherever you want, and you can surround yourself with all the tat you can find in the place.'

'What do you mean, tat? I'll make it a great space.'

'I bet you will.'

'You'll come and visit and not want to leave.'

'I'd do that wherever you were.'

She blushed and looked a little embarrassed. Lee changed the subject quickly, kneeling up on his stool to call, 'Right, who's doing the washing up, then?'

He was met with jeers and catcalls.

Some of them did play cards that night, while snacking on biscuits and cake and drinking coffee in the main area that seemed to have been settled on as the place to hang around. Hester suggested calling it Ground Zero, but Lee's choice of Base Camp met with greater approval. A few sun loungers and a camping chair had been dragged down there to make it more comfortable, and with the lights on, reflecting off the giant crystal feature, it was a magical place to be.

Lee talked to Cozzie for the first time, hearing about her London life, discovering she was a model, although from what she told him he thought she was more of a television extra. Also for the first time, Hester spoke to Claudia, saying how much he loved to holiday in Yorkshire. She raised her eyebrows when he said he was from Kent – she had never been anywhere near Kent, and only thought of the place when her dad watched *The Battle of Britain,* over and over. She asked what he did for a living, and raised her eyebrows again when he rolled off a list of companies that he was a director of. He didn't need a PA, by any chance, did he?

'We'll definitely try to get you out of that doctors' surgery,' he said.

She gave him a stern look. 'How do you know I work in a doctors' surgery?'

'You mentioned it to someone, back in the hotel.'

'Oh, did I?'

Slowly, everyone drifted off to bed, until it was just Lee, Claudia, Leila and Hester. The big man prised himself out of his camping chair with a massive yawn. 'Right, I think I'll retire to my boudoir.'

Claudia bade him good night.

Leila made a move next, kissing Lee on a cheek. 'You won't forget what we're doing in the morning, will you?'

'Of course not. You sleep well.'

He watched her slight frame head up the escalator.

'I'm going too,' Claudia told him. 'I'm shattered.'

'It's all that shoplifting you've done today.'

'Ha-ha. I'll leave you to lock up. Make sure the cat's out.'

He offered his other cheek for a kiss but she gave him a "you'll be lucky" expression.

GB Hope

TEN

'Will! Don't be so fucking stupid!'

Hester paused on the escalator on his way up to find breakfast. It was Cozzie who he could see and hear shouting.

'Cozzie, what's the matter?' he called down.

'That idiot's hitting golf balls around the place.'

Hester smiled and moved on.

Cathy was making toast in McDonald's when the reality of what she was doing finally struck home to her. Thoughts of her family back in the States and of her now ex-fiancé, Mark, moving on with his life without her, caused her to break down in such distress that she almost wet herself and had to crumple to the floor in tears. Hester, in there for his own breakfast, found her by following the howling sound. He helped her sit up on a chair and reached for paper napkins for her tears. He told her to let it all out. She was concerned to be seen by the others but he assured her there was no-one near.

Gradually she calmed down. He squatted there, letting her express all her troubles. She missed Mark more than she could say. She missed her Mom. It was surely a mistake to come to England in these circumstances.

'No, no,' he assured her. 'You know deep down, don't you, that once you're a few weeks into this you'll think it was the right decision. You'll have had a complete break, you'll be refreshed, ready to face new challenges in life. Maybe this Mark bloke will realise what a moron he's been to let you go, and he might be aching for when you get back. Or, you may see it as a blessing, a way to get him out of your system.'

'You are right, I know.'

'Just try to keep busy while you feel like this. It'll work out all right, mark my words.'

She grimly smiled at him using the word "mark".

'Listen, do you want me to eat somewhere else? I don't mind.'

'Oh, certainly not.' She was up on her feet, trying to make herself look respectable. 'Let me help with whatever you're after for your breakfast.'

'That's very good of you, Cathy. See, keeping busy, already.'

She sniffled and smiled at him.

'So, where do we put you, Leila? What do you want? Do you want the austere Vodafone shop, or do you want to be surrounded by fluffy toys in Disney?'

Leila looked straight into Lee's face. 'What does austere mean?'

'It means there's nothing in there but floorboards. Just you and your bed.'

'I don't want to be on show like some freak. Can I have some privacy, please?'

'Well, you need a bigger store, with nooks and crannies.'

'I don't want to be too far away from everyone.'

A pinging sound came near them. They both looked.

'Right,' said Lee. 'I reckon Waterstones, over there, just up the East Blade.'

'Just up the east what?'

'Haven't you heard? This place is set out like a wind turbine, with the three hallways as the blades.'

'Does it matter if I can't get my head round what you just said?'

'Not at all.'

Another pinging ricochet made them turn.

'What *is* that?' asked Leila.

'Oh, I believe Will is playing golf. Come on, let's take a look in Waterstones.'

They walked into the East Blade and entered the book store.

'I don't read much,' she said, before jogging upstairs to look around. 'Maybe I should start.' She came down again and checked out a large alcove with two leather sofas in it. 'If we bring the settees out a bit, a bed can go in there. It'll be cosy,'

'Yeah, if you stretch to the right you can read Hilary Mantel, and to the left you've got... Steve Robinson?'

'Do you like my choice, Lee?'

'I do. I might claim it for myself.'

She gave him a fantastic sulky look. He thought he might have to defend himself.

'You're not having it,' she said. 'You can have the other alcove over there. We could be roomies.'

He was scanning the shelves, thinking that with six

months ahead he could get back into reading, himself. 'I'll give it some thought,' he told her. He moved along sideways. 'What's this one? Dave Clarke, motorcycle travel, *Pack Your Bags And Get Out*. He smiled, thinking how long it would take Leila to say those words to him if they lived together. 'Where are the D's? Ah, here they are.'

'What are you looking for?'

'An ex-girlfriend got her first book published recently. Only because her brother works for the publisher, mind you. Here it is, the piece of shit.'

From his trouser pocket he brought out the cigarette lighter, and proceeded to set fire to the book.

'Lee!' cried Leila. 'What are you doing?'

'It's all right.' He found a metal waste paper bin and dropped the burning volume into it. He watched it burn for a while, then stamped it out with his foot. He looked at Leila. 'What a bitch she was.' He indicated for her to follow him out. 'Come on, let's go and choose your bed.'

She said to him, 'The first time I invite you into my flat and you start setting fire to things.'

Lee spotted Henry. 'Henry! Got a minute? Leila needs a bed moving.'

Henry ran over and joined them in going up to Bedlington's. Leila tried to choose a bed, by flopping down on several of them.

'Come on, Leila,' said Lee. 'We've only got six months.'

'I'll have this one.'

'Get off, then.'

'No, take it with me on it.'

Lee made as if to leave. 'Henry, we're going.'

'No!' squealed Leila, laughing and jumping to her feet.

'This one?' asked Lee. 'Are you sure?'

'Yes, please.'

As the bed was transferred to Waterstones, the pinging sound came again.

'What's that?' asked Henry.

'Will hitting golf balls,' said Lee.

'That kid.'

Leila was installed in the Waterstones alcove. She thanked Henry and he went back to finding his breakfast. Then she gave Lee a full body hug.

'Don't mention it,' he told her, aware of how being in contact with her like that made him feel completely alive. All his previous girlfriends flashed through his mind, with the raunchy Rachel most prominent, but none of them had thrilled him with such electricity as nubile Leila did just there. With a moment to spare before he would become aroused, she let him go and focussed her attention on her new home, as if he wasn't there anymore.

As if remembering his presence, she said, 'You're free to go now, if you like.'

He wanted to take hold of her body again. 'Are you getting rid of me, now you've got what you want?'

'No. I was just being nice. I still need a small table, a lamp, my own towels and toiletries.'

He just stood there and smiled at her.

So they happily spent most of the morning fitting out her bedsit, laughing as he carried a table all the way from Jon Lewis. She made him a sandwich for lunch as a thank you.

'I'm going to lie down after this,' he told her. 'In my

boring dormitory.'

'I did offer you half of my flat.'

As he chewed his dry cheese sandwich, he considered taking her up on her offer. Why shouldn't he? There was only four years between them. It didn't matter if the other people thought it inappropriate. Steady on, he told himself, stay where you are. It was way too early in the game to start getting into things like that.

ELEVEN

The screams jolted everyone out of their afternoon reverie. All heads in Base Camp swivelled in the direction from which they had come. Tony and Hester jumped to their feet. Wailing sounds started to come nearer to them, followed by sobbing and the fast pitter-patter of Cozzie's flip-flops slapping on the marble floor as she ran to the arms of Hester.

Everyone was up and around her, all asking what was wrong.

'Someone down there!' she panted. 'Down near the beer cellar.'

Two hours earlier, Cozzie had gone off to do what she planned to do every day during her incarceration: shop for clothes. Midway through trying on outfits in H&M she had starting thinking about alcohol – not desiring a drink, but wanting to know what the score was. She went on a search, finding nothing in the first few locations; then she found a bar attached to the cinema. There was some booze there, albeit in small quantities and most of it stacked haphazardly on the floor. Unfortunately it was locked behind a metal grille. It was as if they had not gotten round to properly stocking the place. That got her thinking that there would be a larger, accessible store down in the building's underground area. Will, passing on a skateboard, suggested such a place would be down beyond where Tony and Beverley were living. That was where the shopping mall was run from.

She wandered down there, now well-lit but still a cold, unfriendly place compared to the show that was Front of House. She found a little staff canteen, with a gym attached. Then it was all store cupboards and air-conditioning machinery. As she was about to abandon her search, she spotted a stack of metal beer kegs. With a grin, she pushed through heavy rubber doors, immediately seeing a wild-haired man in heavy grey coat sitting in a far corner. He looked up with sunken eyes, on a pale and unshaven face. He was about to speak when she turned and ran screaming.

Hester took charge, telling Madesio and Dr Afridi to stay with the ladies. Tony, Lee and Henry were pointed at with something resembling military signals – they were to back him up.

Downstairs, they found the interloper without too much trouble, mainly because he came walking straight towards them, looking to surrender. Hester gruffly challenged him and the man put up his hands and smiled.

'I won't give you any trouble, lads,' he said. 'Times are bad, you know. I've just been squatting down there for a few weeks.'

'Down where?' asked a suspicious Tony.

'I've got a little room down there. I've been no problem to anyone. While they've been fitting-out the place I've kept a low profile. I've not been nicking anything.'

'What's your name?' asked Hester.

'It's Andrew. Andrew Scholes. I don't want any bother. I'll clear out if you want.'

'You can't clear out,' Lee told him. 'We're all stuck in here for six months.'

'You what?'

'That's right,' said Hester. 'Come on, come up with us. We need to discuss you being here.'

Scruffy Andrew Scholes went where they wanted, with four minders blocking him in at each corner, he didn't really have any choice. The group looked at him as if he were an alien that had landed amongst them.

'Who's this?' asked Beverley.

'A stowaway, apparently,' Tony told her.

'He's been squatting downstairs,' said Lee.

'Hello, all,' said Scholes, looking like he felt he was about to get beaten up, but appealing with his eyes to the females there, nevertheless.

'What are we going to do with him?' asked Claudia.

'Get rid of him,' spat Cozzie.

Hester hugged Cozzie by the shoulder. 'You're such a sweetheart. We can't get rid of him, I'm afraid.'

Scholes decided it was best to keep talking. 'I heard you all arrive. I didn't think you'd be staying. So, what are you doing, market research, or something? Are you testing the place out?'

'Something like that,' answered Henry. 'Why don't we send him the same way as the wheelbarrow?'

'Steady on, Henry,' said Tony. 'We've not known anything about him, have we? He'll have to go off and keep himself to himself again somewhere.'

'Until he comes out and cuts our throats at night,' said Cozzie.

'Hey!' Scholes protested. 'I'm not dangerous. Any one of these guys might harm you ahead of me, lady. If I really can't get out, then you won't hear another peep out of me.'

It was Lee who took the heat out of the situation. 'People. We're all just a bit surprised. We didn't expect this. But what would that Frankie man say? Mr Scholes here has survived in his own way, now he's joined our group.'

'He's not joined my group,' insisted Cozzie.

'Well,' continued Lee, 'I'm sure Mr Scholes will go off to a part of the building and not bother us again.'

'No fear on that score,' said Scholes.

Most people returned to their seats. Beverley enquired if Scholes was hungry. Hester, Lee and Tony went into a huddle to decide what was for the best. If their own circumstances had been even remotely normal they might have invited Scholes to become part of the group, but seeing as he was a tramp and a squatter, they thought it best to banish him. As long as he could take care of himself, it should be all right.

In the end, the three of them walked Scholes and his mangy possessions to the far end of the West Blade, where he had his own food outlet, a furniture store to crash in, and his own toilet facilities. He appeared delighted with the developments, thanking them profusely, for what amounted to being treated like a leper.

'So, you'll stay around here, then?' asked Hester, with a touch of menace in his voice.

'Definitely, guvnor. This will do me just grand.'

As they walked away, Lee felt it strange that they would not care to interact with a fellow human being even briefly, just as if a zombie plague had in fact struck the country. He glanced back once more, seeing Andrew Scholes still waving.

Over the next few days, Dr Afridi visited Scholes a couple of times, reporting back that he found him in excellent health for someone in his difficult personal circumstances, and that he was content with his lot in life.

And then they all tried to forget him for a while.

GB Hope

TWELVE

Hester was still chatting to everyone when he got the chance
– not about anything of great importance – he was just a bit
like one of those tough uncles you feel you could go round
and tell your problems to, while in the back of your mind
you knew he would crack a few skulls for you if things got
out of hand. They all guessed that he was the wealthiest
amongst them. Perhaps that helped to ease any reservations
about opening up to him. Surely, he must have lived through
many things and dealt with all sorts. It was good that he was
there with them.

Suddenly, the days were flying by. Routines had formed
for the duration, eating when and where it pleased them,
finding ways to entertain themselves or taking part in
exercise. Bicycles became popular, and Will became the bike
supplier, bringing around different models for them all to
try out. Lee was fussy, though, going over to JD Sports to
choose his own, without interference, coming back with a
very expensive black mountain bike. Lee started racing Will
on their bikes, up and down levels, until Will came off his
bike and almost put himself through the front window of the
Disney store. Dr Afridi gave them both a stern telling off.

In the middle of the second week they had a mini-football tournament with nets dragged out of a sports shop, but that descended into anarchy. Next, there was a shopping trolley race, the men pushing, with the girls as passengers. Lee won, but had to accept he had the lightest partner in Leila. Then, they held a badminton competition. Cathy, who they cheerfully accused of being semi-professional at the sport, beat all-comers. 'Americans!' they called. 'Have to win at everything!' Tony found the best trophy in the sports shop and presented it to her during the evening meal.

Lee moved out of the Homeware dormitory, not into Waterstones with Leila, but across the way into Thorntons. The luxury sweet shop was one of the few places without any stock, which was quite annoying. He made his bed behind big cardboard adverts for treacle toffee. He and Leila shared the working shower in the nearby bathroom showroom, and they enjoyed being neighbours. If they had lunch or coffee together it would be on her leather sofas. Occasionally, in the evenings, they would even read books in there. She started on the first ever Harry Potter and he was on *Layer Cake* by JJ Connolly. He'd seen the film with his favourite actor, Daniel Craig, and thought the crime novel to be just as good, although he almost threw it away early on when, on page six, some characters "met at the wedding of Clarkie's creamy younger sister" and then on page eight "Clarkie was the youngest of his family". He wondered if someone somewhere in publishing got disciplined for not spotting that error.

Unlike his own gaff in Thorntons, Leila had made the place interesting and homely, with cushions from BHS and ornaments from Jon Lewis. There were also framed images of Marilyn Monroe and Noel Gallagher taken from one of those memorabilia/autograph shops.

They had by no means broken off from the others. There were no cliques forming, everyone was still in it together. Claudia and Henry found they were talking more. She had completely forgotten her joke in the hotel about not being able to get through six months without having a man. If she did get to that stage, then the athletic Henry would be in the top three, of course – the choice not being that great to start with. She just found him less laddish, less of a typical builder, now that he had to adapt to the slow way of life inside the mall. The two of them, as well as Cozzie, were the only ones to seek out a drink in the evening, but they kept their behaviour in moderation.

In week three, Andrew Scholes made his presence known again. In his area, he had a major games store, and had taken to playing on either of the huge X-Box and Playstation systems with their wall-sized screens and cinema-surround sound. At night the noise carried all the way to the others. Nobody bothered to go along and ask him to keep it down. When he wasn't playing video games, he had found a dart board. Word filtered back to the others that he was playing darts for up to seven hours a day.

'He must want to turn professional,' joked Tony.

A number of people laughed.

'I warned you he was nuts,' said Cozzie.

After Dr Afridi, a little bored actually, walked over to check on him again, he reported back that Scholes was trying to do his own version of a nine-dart finish. He knew he could never get two 180's followed by a treble 20, a treble 19 and a double 12. So he'd set himself to get two 100's and then two trebles, finishing on the double 12. Apparently, in thousands of attempts, he had got as far as the final treble 19 on two occasions.

Cozzie said, 'That might explain those two howls we heard. Is he mentally ill, or what, doctor?'

'Not necessarily. Perfectly sane people practise sport obsessively. Look at golf, or snooker. I'll keep an eye on him, though.'

Scholes became a tourist attraction on their bike rides – "There's Scholesy, playing his darts."

Scholes, however, did give up on the games console – while happily engaged in a 24hr endurance race, he was shocked to realise that there was something unexpected up ahead of him on the road. He slowed his speed dramatically, but still there came a succession of loud thuds as he drove through something. Only when he was down to 20 mph did he understand that there were hordes of zombies, a wall of moving flesh that he was still hitting and feeling bounce off his car. Dumbstruck, he let the controller drop between his feet, watched the bizarre image for a moment longer, then went away to do something else with his time.

Leila told Lee she thought she was getting fat, and asked if he would start jogging with her. He stepped back a pace and looked with all seriousness at her slender figure and told her she was off her rocker.

Her face dropped. 'Will you not jog with me, then?'

'Of course, I'll jog with you.'

They raided one of the sports shops for running gear and agreed on a gentle run-out the following morning. By that moment in the confinement, things to do were always "in the morning" or "tomorrow afternoon" because they had all quickly lost track of what day it was.

Finally getting adventurous, Lee chose a yellow Adidas tracksuit and went calling on Leila. 'Leila, are you coming out to play?'

She ran out to him and his jaw almost hit the floor. The largest item of clothing on her entire body were her Nike cross-trainers. Over her small bust sat a black sports boob-tube thing and her black shorts were so tight that even her sexily thin and smooth legs were bulging at the top of her thighs. She asked if he was ready to go jogging. Never mind jogging, he thought, he was ready to take her back into her alcove and have his way with her.

'Let's go,' he forced himself to say.

They moved off at a slow trot. As surreptitiously as he could, he managed to appraise her glowing, vitally healthy body, her beautiful skin just off-white. It prompted him to ask where she thought her roots were in the world, and not to say Southport. She said she didn't know.

'Leila?'

'Yes?'

'You're a total hottie.'

'Thank you, I know. Will you exercise with me every day, then?'

'I will.'

They went by where Cozzie and Claudia were shopping in Gap. Everyone waved. Lee thought it a particularly surreal moment.

'Leila?' he said.

'Yes?'

'You are over sixteen, aren't you?'

'Yes, why?'

'What year were you born?'

'What are you, a pub landlord? I was born on May 13th, 2000.'

'May 13th?'

'Yes.'

'Really, May 13th?'

'Why would I lie about my birthday? Why are you getting excited? What's May 13th mean to you, anyway?'

'May 13th, 2012, the Etihad stadium in Manchester. Man City win their first title in forty-four years with two amazing injury-time goals, when all City fans thought they had blown it as usual. And to deny Man United in the process. It's the greatest day of my life.'

She was totally underwhelmed by that news. 'Oh. The greatest day of your life? Well, on May 13th from now on you can remember when you met me.'

'You've got a high opinion of yourself.'

'Too right I have.'

'Well, I'm not sure I'll be able to add you to my May 13th memories.'

'Do I need to convince you?'

'Yes, I think you may need to do that.'

THIRTEEN

Will desisted from hitting golf balls all around the mall, not through any sense of respect for the other people there, it was just that he came across a better place to use his driver. He showed Henry what he had found. On the roof above one of the sports shops there was a single, green acrylic, tennis court, enclosed with a mesh fence.

'Hey, this is wicked,' said Henry. 'Let's have a go.' He teed up a ball with the driver and launched it into the fence. He tried again, this time the ball soared off the roof. 'What we need is a spotter, to see if we hit any zombies.'

When Hester heard of the tennis court, he rushed straight up to see it. At home in Kent, and at his Miami beach house retreat, he had his own courts and was a massive tennis fan. He was delighted and went immediately to kit himself out in the full Adidas gear and to pick out half a dozen racquets. Tony and Beverley shared his enthusiasm for the sport and were happy to go up there to play him.

Everyone else eventually levitated towards the sun trap on the roof to watch the tennis entertainment. Beverley made a gallon of a fruit drink, not exactly Pimms, but very refreshing. Hester managed to coerce most of them to play him. He even made out a rota, as if he were arranging to have duels with them: Lee in one hour's time, Cozzie straight after that, Claudia following the evening meal, Henry after breakfast the following day, etc, etc.

Hester beat Lee 6-0, 6-0. It wasn't that Lee didn't know one end of a racket from the other – he, like his friends, had pretended on many occasions to be Rafa Nadal or Andy Murray down the local park as a child, and he was fit and athletic. It was just that Hester was so very good. Hester showed no mercy, but he was impressed with the way Lee kept trying his best and refused to lose heart at all, even as he was continually passed.

Cozzie was very sporty, playing in a black and yellow Kappa tracksuit. She was London's answer to Venus Williams. She managed to lose 6-2, 6-2.

Into a cooler evening, Claudia came up in full tennis gear, including a Nike peaked headband, causing great hilarity amongst the watching crowd. 'Wey-hey!' called Lee, 'It's Ana Ivanovic!' Claudia smiled and curtseyed. She called something about playing for the county at junior level, but still only took five games off the obsessive Hester.

This guy likes to win, thought Lee, sitting with a glass of Beverley's punch brought over to him by Leila. 'Will you be having a go?' he asked her.

'I'm booked for tomorrow morning.'

He laughed. 'I'm surprised you're not being a ball girl.'

'Piss off.'

'I can't wait to see you play.'

'Well, I can't be any worse than you, can I?'

They smiled at each other. He looked at her smooth legs

emerging from denim shorts, her bare feet adorably turned inwards.

'You be wearing a really short skirt?'

'If you want me to, you perv'.'

The one person so far not to have sat down for a chat with Hester was Lee. They found themselves alone one morning, having coffee in Base Camp.

'What do you do, Hester? For a living, I mean?'

'Fabrics, mostly. I have a lot of interests, a lot of shares in various businesses, properties. Would you like to join my stable after all this? I could use a capable man like yourself.'

'You're making me feel like I'm on *The Apprentice*. I do want to change the direction of my life, but right now I've switched off. Do you know what I mean? It would upset me to even think about work and a career.'

'I understand completely. Everyone needs a holiday from life at least once.'

'How are you coping with this? Sorry, have you got a wife?'

'I've got three. Technically, just the current Mrs Hester at the moment. Two divorcees, but I can't get rid of them.' He smiled. 'I'll have to get myself out to Utah, so I can have three or four at the same time.'

'Is that still allowed? Sounds more trouble than it's worth to me.'

'Well, the modern way doesn't really work either, does it? What is it, the divorce rate, at the moment? Must be massively high.'

'That's the economy as well, though. People are less likely

to stick together if they're always arguing about money.'

'Yes, money. Money is a terrible invention.'

Lee grinned and leant back in his seat – the rich guy bemoaning money. He looked up towards the underneath of the observation dome, high above the Base Camp.

'Hester, do you fancy an expedition? Could we find our way into the dome? See what we can see out there.'

'That sounds like a cracking idea to me.' He stepped into his boots. 'Let's make a plan. Will we need anything?'

'Certainly not a torch, it's brighter than the sun up there. Tools, we might have to break a lock. Binoculars to take in the view.'

'I don't know where we'd find binoculars, but we can pick up a couple of crowbars from the DIY store on the way up.'

'Shall we go, then?'

'Lead the way, young man.'

They picked up the jemmies, as well as a hanger-on in the form of Leila. Upstairs, they searched for staff entrances or a separate lift. Leila spotted the way up, through the back of the crystal feature. They had to break through a small panel, duck inside, and then work their way up a metal spiral staircase, like Knights attacking a castle keep, leading with their blood-red crowbars. They were faced with a more substantial door at the top. There was a keypad on the wall which they, of course, didn't bother pressing. Lee examined the doorframe, thought he could force it with a great deal of effort. He put the crowbar in place and began heaving on it.

'Shall I go and get Henry?' asked Leila, taking the mickey.

'We'll get there,' he told her.

It took fifteen minutes of both men going at the door and the surrounding plasterwork, with light starting to filter through the damage they were creating.

'It's going!' shouted Lee, his shoulder to the stiff door. He barged it again and it opened six to ten inches. Then he almost had a heart attack as something rushed forward and collapsed into his legs, forcing him to the floor and pinning him there as he swore and shouted and kicked out. Leila screamed at the same time. Hester dropped down to his knees to try to drag Lee clear.

Lee was in the grasp of a robotic zombie. The initial shock dissipated quickly, but he was still being held by a machine that pulsed and rocked as it tried to carry out the role it had been programmed for.

'For fuck's sake.' said Lee, not being hurt in any way, or even distressed, just sweating profusely and annoyed to be held down in such a fashion. His trousers were being torn and his boots badly damaged. A man could take it, he thought, but he was glad Leila's bare legs were not in the machine's grasp. 'What's this all about? It's like having a horny Rottweiler trying to shag my leg.'

Hester was trying to kick and punch the machine but it refused to budge. While in the space above Lee, he saw other zombies moving around the well-lit glass dome area. Leila offered to get Henry again, seriously that time, but Hester held her by her hips. 'Leila, sweetheart, stay with Lee. I'll be back in ten minutes to sort this out.'

'Okay,' she said.

'Lee, stay calm,' said Hester. 'I won't be long.'

With that, he left them in that bizarre situation. Leila

used a tissue to mop Lee's brow. Then she sat down close to him. Lee, very unhappy to have a machine mauling his leg, still managed to smile at her. She shrugged her shoulders and offered him some chewing gum.

'What are you thinking?' he asked.

'Just wondering how long I'm going to give this.'

He laughed. 'Leila, you're priceless.'

Hester was back fairly quickly, himself sweating like a pig, and now toting the rifle from out of the post box.

'Where the fuck is that from?' asked Lee.

'I'll explain in a minute. Stay still! Leila, stand over there.'

Lee's eyes were popping out of his head. 'Hester...'

Hester had already loaded the rifle downstairs. He put the muzzle up against the robot zombie's head and squeezed the trigger. The bang was shocking in such a confined space. Hester had made a mess of the zombie, but it still clawed at Lee's legs. He fired again and the machine dropped away with a loud hissing sound and a small plume of smoke. Finding himself free, Lee withdrew his leg and stood up, relieved not to have been electrocuted. Leila moved back in to hold him.

'Hester,' said Lee. But Hester was aiming again and firing off at the other zombies that seemed to have a circuit around the circular dome. When he was convinced he was done, he lowered the rifle and they had to push into the dome just to get away from all the gun smoke.

'It's a gun to shoot zombies in the car-park,' explained Hester, once they had all caught their breath.

Lee didn't know what to say. The rifle was being swung

onto Hester's shoulder by the strap - the big white hunter. They all took a moment to calm down. Lee still had Leila in contact with him. She was not frightened at all, he noticed. He kissed her right temple and moved away to look out through the panoramic windows. As suspected, most of the view was farmland, but sitting there was the nearby town, looking quite large, spreading off into a summer haze.

'Seems like England to me,' said Hester.

Lee looked at him. 'What, you thought we might have been drugged on the bus and flown overseas?'

'It was a possibility.'

'Well, that's Berkshire for me, and I'd quite like to be in that town right now.'

'Come on, Lee, don't you want to go out on the roof and shoot zombies? I know Leila does.'

Lee looked at Leila nodding enthusiastically. He had to laugh.

'What a fucking madhouse!' he joked.

They had a good wash and helped themselves to cold drinks by smashing into a vending machine. Hester checked the rifle, then covered it with a large towel for the journey to the roof above Jon Lewis. When they got out up there they found Claudia and Cathy sunbathing, prostrate on their backs on lounger cushions. Following Hester up, Lee had wondered why the man had excused himself. It was a pleasantly shocking sight to see the two women in just their underwear – as they had not bothered to find swimsuits.

Claudia propped herself up on her elbows, wearing large dark sunglasses that helped place her back into the Claudia

Cardinale era.

'Sunglasses Hut?' asked Lee, joking to mask his interest in their semi-nakedness.

'You're right. Do you like them?'

'I do. Very fetching.'

Of course, he was wallowing in the image of her body again. Then he looked at Cathy. The American was less toned than Claudia, but still very sexy in her white "bikini".

'Don't mind us,' he said. 'We're just going to shoot zombies.'

Hester had moved a little way off, but he was still admiring the sunbathing women. Cathy sat up at the mention of shooting. Neither of the two men had realised before how perfect her breasts were. She had always been the pretty but prim American lady. Now she had her own fan club. As if realising this, she reached for a white cotton kaftan dress by her side and slipped it on.

The rifle was visible by then. Both girls expressed surprise, but in a positive way.

'You know your way around a rifle, Cathy?' asked Hester.

'Well, not a rifle,' she replied, getting to her feet. 'But I own a Glock 9mm back home.'

Claudia laughed at that typical American trait. She stood up without making any attempt to get dressed and went to see the rifle.

During these exchanges, Leila had a face on her like the moody teenager she was, clearly envious of Claudia's figure and the effect it had on Lee. But when Hester was about to take his first shot at a zombie she cheered up and took her position to the side of them.

The zombies still wandered aimlessly back and forth across the car-park. For their entertainment, he told them to watch one in a red shirt over to the right. He lifted the rifle, rearranged the strap around his elbow as if he had done that kind of thing for many years and took aim. With a crack he took down the zombie with a shot to the back of the head. A smiling Cathy applauded him and Claudia whooped. He took two more shots, only staggering one zombie and missing the other. Laughing, he let Cathy have a go. That annoyed Leila, but she kept quiet. Lee noticed and ruffled her hair, which annoyed her even more.

Cathy wounded one zombie and missed two.

'Leila's next,' called Lee.

'Go on, Leila,' said Claudia.

Leila stepped into the middle of them all, almost too slim to wield the big rifle.

'The kick's not too bad,' said Hester, his hand now on her lower back as he guided the rifle to her right shoulder. 'Just be prepared for it.'

Leila fired. A hit! A zombie toppling forward, cheers all round. She fired again and got another one to fall. Lee was immensely proud of her. Then she missed. He gave her a playful boo and she slapped his arm as Hester took away the rifle.

Hester offered the rifle to Lee. He found it an extraordinary experience. He tried to remember if he had ever shot anything before, apart from his six-year-old niece cruelly with a Nerf water gun. He took aim, for what seemed like an age, and fired.

'I can't say I noticed anything out there,' joked Claudia.

He fired twice more without troubling the scorers. 'Bugger! Come on, Claudia, your turn.'

Claudia took deep breaths before the rifle came to her. Lee felt Leila move up against him. She asked softly, 'Can I have another go?'

'Of course. I'll ask Hester how many bullets we've got.'

Lee held the young Leila close and watched sexy Claudia from York, in only her knickers and bra, firing a rifle at robotic zombies off the roof of a shopping centre. He wondered, shaking his head, if life could possible get any better than that.

FOURTEEN

Treble twenty. Treble twenty. Single twenty. Stage one done. Head still, point dart up, lower slowly, release quickly. Keep it smooth. Keep it smooth. Treble twenty – yes. Treble twenty – yes. Single one – that's allowed. It's on! Treble twenty – yes! Treble nineteen – yes! Stay cool. Don't be low. Don't be low. Up, lower, release. Fucking low!! Fucking hell!! Jesus fucking Christ!!

The day after the rifle shooting, Cathy returned to the roof to continue her sunbathing. She listened to songs on her new MP3 player, everything from *Adele* to *Tone Loc*, making sure not to play any that reminded her of Mark back home in Buffalo. She had spoken to Hester again about the break-up, and felt less distraught deep within herself. Perhaps the trip to England had been the right idea, after all. No doubt in the coming months she would slip back and feel sorry for herself again, but at that moment the strangeness of the vacation was sustaining her.

A shadow moved over her face as Tony came up to look at the world. She covered herself with the white Kaftan dress that she loved and sat up. He apologised for disturbing her.

She pulled out the earplugs. 'Sorry?'

'I just said, sorry to have bothered you.'

'It's no problem.'

He looked around, breathing in the air deeply. He noticed the downed zombies amongst their perpetually moving colleagues. 'They're starting to fail, I see.'

She decided not to mention the rifle shooting. 'Apparently.'

The weather was hot, but there was a beautiful breeze up there.

'Quite pretty countryside,' he stated. 'Not a patch on Yorkshire, though.'

'Beverley said you two have a guest house in Malton. I'm sure it's a beautiful place.'

'It's certainly that. Have you ever been to Yorkshire?'

'Ah, can I answer yes and no to that? I've never been there, but my ancestors came originally from Yorkshire.'

'Did they really? I can look at you in a new light now – one of God's own people. You should definitely go there after this.'

'It's on my to-do list. But I might be desperate to be Stateside after six months locked in here.'

'How are you coping with it?'

'I suppose as well as everyone else. You?'

'Me? Well, don't tell Bev, but I did eight months in prison while I was in my twenties – handling stolen goods, nothing serious. Doing time in here is pure heaven to me.'

'Well, it's certainly an experience, I'll say that.'

'Have you wondered why you were chosen for this?'

'No, I've not thought about it.'

'I don't know why me and Beverley were picked, either. It's just, to bring you all the way over the Atlantic. I find it strange, that's all.'

'Perhaps,' she mused, 'some of the people behind this have a US connection. Maybe they'll do the same thing over there, and take a couple of Brits along.'

'For another hundred grand I'm in for that gig as well, I can tell you.'

'Well, I'm glad you're on this one. I think all the people here are very nice.'

'I'm not sure of a couple, myself, but you're certainly in the positive group.'

'Thank you. Tony, you see that house over there, beyond the wall?'

'I see it.'

'I thought I saw someone on the roof earlier.'

'Did you?' He strained for a better look. 'Nobody there now. It's probably not connected to us.'

Proof that they had not been drugged on the coach and taken to another country, that they were, in fact, in England during summertime, came that afternoon when the weather completely switched and a cold storm front moved in.

It immediately affected everyone's mood, to be living under the artificial lights during the day, with rain lashing the roof at all points, only grey darkness to be seen up above. People ate more, became grumpy, a few arguments sprang up. Beverley and Tony had a disagreement and retired to their room to thrash it out. Hester decided to go back to his bed. Cathy took a mug of cocoa and some magazine to hide away in the girls' dorm.

Even Lee and Leila fell out, over his apparent lack of interest in finding a new sport to play in the afternoon. Cozzie got involved from her seat in Base Camp, telling the younger girl to let the man be. Lee quickly got to his feet as he could see the change in Leila's eyes. He got there just in time to deflect her attempt to scratch Cozzie's face to shreds, ending up with the three of them grappling and falling over chairs, and having to be separated by the others. Leila ran off and wasn't seen for the rest of the day.

After a couple of hours of torrential downpour, it was Madesio who noticed the water coming in. It was not of any great concern to the small group who went around the ground floor to examine the state of affairs – it was just making the floors wet. It was certainly something that shouldn't happen.

'Piss-poor building standards?' offered Lee.

'I can't see that,' said Henry. 'A place like this would be checked at every stage of construction. I'm thinking it's more likely deliberate.'

'Another aspect of the game?' asked Dr Afridi. 'Letting the rain in? Can it get any worse?'

It rained non-stop for three days and did get worse. There was no threat to safety, there was just an inch of water sloshing around everywhere downstairs. They had to put chairs on tables and transfer Base Camp up to outside McDonald's. It stopped their cycling around and made them change their footwear to splash from place to place. The men sleeping in the Homeware store were fine, because that seemed to slope upwards where they were sleeping. Hester and Lee in their respective flats put up with the inconvenience for the time being. They created sand bags from one of the children's stores and mopped up as best they could inside. They agreed that if it worsened, then they would relocate upstairs. As soon as the problem developed, Lee went in search of Leila and they put her bed up on the second level in Waterstones. She was upset with herself for causing their falling out. She was humbly grateful that he had thought to come to her rescue. She kissed him on the mouth. He had not been expecting it, so it had been a very one-sided kiss, but cute in its own way. She blushed a little.

'Are we friends again?' she asked.

'It was never in doubt. Are you settled up here now?'

'It's lovely. Thank you. Will this flooding stop you coming to visit?'

'Of course not. I'll come by canoe if it gets any worse.'

As it turned out, the days of the flood boosted morale. They were all kitted out in Wellington boots, and just got on with it. It was the Blitz spirit, although that had to be explained to Madesio. And still it rained. Lounging about upstairs in Waterstones, Leila surprised Lee by expressing concern for the car-park zombies.

'Babe, they'd gobble your leg if they got a chance.'

'I just wonder if they've stopped moving.'

'Shall we go up to the dome and see?'

She was giddily excited about that. She looked about her for her six pairs of designer boots from which to choose from, picked some, checked her hair in a mirror and followed him out. Unobserved by anyone, they re-opened the panel in the crystal feature and went up the spiral staircase. They found it gloomy up there, walking around the remnants of the zombies Hester had dealt with to check the sky from all points of the compass. There was some hope of respite from the weather in the western sky.

'Look, your zombies are still moving, Leila.'

'Oh, good. I'm pleased about that.'

They lounged there together against the outer wall, watching the town with streetlights on and some movement of cars on the roads. Perhaps subconsciously he found himself playing with the thin fingers of her hands that had been entwined with his, appraising her nails and then moving down to examine her thin veins in her wrists.

''I'm sorry,' he said.

'I don't mind.'

He kissed the back of one of her hands and she beamed up at him and snuggled in closer. He looked down into her face, wanting to kiss her, not sure why he just didn't get on and do it. Maybe it was the bizarre situation, the place. Maybe he was waiting for a scantily-clad Claudia to show up.

'Would you mind kissing me?' Leila asked.

That solved the problem. He obliged, and they remained kissing for a long time, up there in the dome, with rain swirling around them.

The weather brightened up after four days. Slowly the mall started to dry out. Beverley embarked on a cleaning frenzy, and also came up with a better system for trash removal. Hester and Lee disinfected the wooden floors of their flats, then they teamed up to look at Leila's home. The problem was the carpet which had been saturated. It needed to be stripped out. They told her she'd have to move. She cried right there in front of them. Hester found that extraordinary, Lee just hugged her. To Leila they had sounded like the officialdom who always dealt with her when her mother was in trouble with the law, shunting her around the North-West of England.

'Shush,' Lee comforted her in a whisper. 'We'll find you somewhere just as good.'

'I don't want to go,' she whispered back, not wanting Hester to hear. 'I want to be near you.'

'You will be. I promise.' He turned to Hester. 'We'll have to go looking.'

'Okay, shout me if you need me.'

'Cheers, Hester.'

Prompted perhaps by Lee expressing his gratitude, Leila skipped over to hug Hester. 'Thank you.'

'The pleasure's all mine, young lady.'

Hester left them to it. They squelched out of Waterstones to assess their options.

'You know,' she said. 'When my brother had a flat in Southport, he got flooded out once by the girl upstairs. His mate put him up for a few weeks until the damage was repaired.'

'Leila, if you want me to put you up on my couch, I'll have to get one first.'

'I'll sleep in with you.'

'Will you now? What will the others think?'

He realised that she had no comprehension of what their

fellow mall-mates would think if she shacked up with him. Then he wondered why he was bothered; when did he get so conservative all of a sudden? Leila was a total darling, and probably only eighteen months younger than Rachel back in Liverpool.

But then Leila saw Lipsy of London, her favourite women's wear shop, two doors down from Thorntons, and he was suddenly annoyed to have passed up the chance to have her in his bed. She dragged him over to it.

'I didn't know this was here,' she said. 'I've come home. I can live amongst the best clothes.' Lee was thinking of calling for Hester – the wooden floor would have to be cleaned. 'I want my Waterstones sofas brought over, though.'

'Oh, of course. You should be...' He was going to say "in my bed for all the work I'm doing for you", but he finished with, 'very happy here.'

'Thanks, Lee.'

FIFTEEN

Exercise resumed in the mall. Will and Henry took to kicking a football about, but well away from Cozzie's sharp tongue. Lee and Leila returned to their jogging. Madesio and Dr Afridi found a rowing machine in one of the sports shops, while most of the others continued to enjoy their bike rides.

Cathy, aware that a few of the men were taking an interest in her, especially as she looked tanned and healthy, joined in the discussion when Madesio talked about how far he had rowed that day. He invited her to join them "the following morning", which she did, but the rowing machine seemed quite insane to her. Instead, she found a pretend horse-riding contraption, basically a saddle and pommel machine which mimicked the movements of the horse, and thought that simply perfect. It was supposed to tone her up around the inner thigh and buttock area. She looked a bit ludicrous, though, moving up and down at the back of the store, and became somewhat of an attraction, like Andrew Scholes.

Then Madesio found something that fascinated and horrified everyone without exception. It was positioned just before Jon Lewis in the North Blade – a sports/adventure shop that nobody had ever heard of. It had gone unnoticed because the way up to the roof was right there. Inside, there were video games and adventure holiday brochures everywhere. Right in the centre of the store there stood a ten ft square cubicle and inside that, at first impression, there was some kind of drilling platform, metal and plastic, fifteen feet tall. The base of the cubicle could be walked on, even though it was a type of HD screen.

Henry and Hester found the way to power up the machine. The floor beneath the drilling derrick came alive with moving colours, mainly blue. They all walked around it, trying to figure it out.

'That's a river,' decided Cozzie.

Oh, shit.' said Tony. 'I think you're supposed to be seeing that in 3D, while hanging upside down on that thing.'

'*What*, Tony?' asked Cathy, gawping at him.

'You know, I think he's right,' said Hester.

Hester made the image change to one of vehicles moving along an American street, with little yellow taxi cabs scuttling across.

'Yes,' continued Tony. 'Once you're in that, with 3D glasses on, it rotates down, and you have, my friends, a virtual bungee jump.'

Will spun away clapping his hands and laughing with the sheer fun of the idea. Beverley and Dr Afridi moved away for a different reason – the sheer horror of it. Everyone was looking at each other, seeing who fancied having a go. Claudia looked at Lee and laughed.

'Have you done that for real?' he asked. 'Tough Yorkshire lass like you.'

'Don't be ridiculous. Have you?'

'Ah! Well, actually, no. I've been under one in a pub car-park before, though. I watched the local nutters do it.'

'Here are the 3D glasses,' said Leila, offering them to Lee.

'What are you giving them to me for?' he asked, aghast. She laughed.

The glasses were more like a baseball helmet, only with covers for both ears, not just the one liable to get struck by the ball.

'Well, come on,' said Leila. 'It's not as if it's real.'

'Well, I think it will feel pretty real, and still make my heart explode.'

'Come on, Lee,' teased Claudia.

'Let Tony go first, he's the expert.'

Tony laughed and agreed. Beverley stood nearby with her arms crossed as her husband was strapped to the machine's cradle, as if he was going to be spun in one of those human gyroscopes.

'I'll keep hiding behind the machine,' joked Hester. 'I might not have to have a go, then. I think I know how it works, mind you.'

Henry had gone quite pale. His mates had done that kind of thing before on holiday beaches, but he had always bluffed his way out. 'I'm not keen on this. Get Scholesy, he can have my turn.'

Everyone stepped out and watched the action through side panels in the cubicle.

'Here we go!' shouted Hester. 'Bungee over raging river, it says here, apparently. Tony, it seems you have to verbally say "good to go". Must be a legal requirement.'

'Good to go!' screamed Tony.

The cradle slowly rotated forward so that Tony was head over heels, and that was as exciting as it got for the spectators outside. Tony screamed even louder and made all kinds of "whoa!" sounds, but he didn't actually go anywhere.

'This is a bit like watching motor racing,' said Madesio. 'Probably better if you're taking part.'

Cathy held him by the arm. 'Are you going next?'

'I wasn't planning on going at all. Should I? It's safe, clearly. No, no, it's a crazy thing.'

'Come on, Madesio. What would they say back in New York if you chickened out?'

Everyone decided the issue for him – Madesio was next up. Tony emerged, completely exhilarated, swearing under his breath at how alive he felt, rushing over to embrace Beverley and try to talk her into having a go. 'You see it coming up at you,' he was saying, 'but you know it's safe. It all rushes at you, and you hear it in your ears. Try it, darling. You'll love it.' Everyone found it amusing watching her vehemently refuse to even entertain the notion.

Claudia, excited, took hold of Henry round his waist. 'You will do it, won't you, Henry? It's not real. No rope's going to break.'

In the end, about half of them went bungee-jumping. Madesio, of course, picked the American street. Cathy and Leila chose to go off the Golden Gate bridge, Lee down to a crocodile infested river. Henry screamed "Good to go!" and didn't have a clue where he went. Will, until Hester became bored, did most of what the computer had to offer.

The ones brave enough to do the bungee jumping, except

Tony who followed Beverley downstairs, went up to the roof in high spirits, to laugh and joke and celebrate surviving the experience. Cathy and Madesio sat down on her sunbathing mat to recover their cool.

'Wasn't that great?' she said to him. 'Well done you for finding that place.'

'Thank you. It's amazing what they can do these days. Would you like me to get some drinks?'

'In a minute.'

Lee was delighted at how happy it had made Leila. 'How brave are you?' he said to her.

She was beaming at him. 'That was brilliant. Can we do it again some time? What were the crocodiles like when you got down there?'

'I thought they were going to snap my head off! Hey, me Tarzan! You, Jane!' He tried to pick her up and put her over his shoulder but she playfully screamed and fended him off.

'I'm sweating like a pig,' she told him. 'I'm going for a shower.'

'Am I invited?'

'Don't be rude.'

After the evening meal, the same members of the new daredevil club reassembled on the roof with coffee and a variety of cakes. Cozzie was there as someone's guest. With it being a lovely summer's evening, some of them had brought up chairs or big cushions. Will had carried up a large, black bean bag from the Next store and was happily ensconced in that, with ginger biscuits and a cup of tea. Lee could make out the aroma of barbecues wafting on the air, and wondered if there was some kind of holiday out there in the real world. For a second, he thought of Rachel, the first melancholic feelings for the girlfriend, but then a refreshed Leila hugged him from behind.

'Hello, you,' she said.

'Hello, yourself.'

'If we had some music, we could have a party.'

'I could sing, if you like.'

'No, you're all right. Come and sit with me.'

Leila was wearing her hair in pigtails, and the crop top she had chosen, revealing her bare midriff, made Lee consider her to be both innocent and horny at the same time. They sat and nibbled the cookies she had brought out, watching the sun start to go down. Lee noticed Henry trying his luck with Claudia again, but she had regained her composure since the bungee-jumping and didn't seem too keen – in fact, it seemed a chore for her to look at him as he wittered on.

Cathy and Madesio were close to the edge, watching the zombies move around.

'Hey, guys!' called Madesio. 'Guys, come over here.' They all got up and joined them. 'Look over there.'

He was pointing to the house which was nearest to the mall car-park. There was a figure on the roof, waving a white board above his head.

'I knew there was somebody there!' said Cathy. 'I saw something the other day.'

'What's he doing?' asked Cozzie.

'It's a message,' said Henry.

Lee turned to Leila. 'Have you not brought your

binoculars up?'

'Stop it.'

Lee asked Madesio, 'What shop would have binoculars? A sports shop?'

'More likely a camera one.'

'I'll go,' volunteered Henry, rushing inside.

While he was gone, they milled about on the roof, speculating wildly. Will's contribution to the discussion was, 'He's probably just calling us a bunch of tossers.'

'That'll be the one,' joked Lee.

As they faced out towards the mystery man, Lee held Leila from behind and rested his chin on her right shoulder. No-one seemed to notice or particularly care about the touching that was going on between them, so Lee clasped his hands together just above the very low-slung belt of her hipster jeans. She did notice, though, and clamped her hands over his as if to make sure they weren't removed.

Henry came back panting, passing a pair of binoculars to Lee like a baton in a race. Lee extricated himself from Leila and attempted to focus with them on the house, his eyes wandering all over the zombies and then the fence. 'Where is he? There he is.'

'What's he saying?' asked Leila.

Lee turned the little wheel on top of the binoculars to be able to make out the man. It was definitely a stranger to him. He panned up to read the sign:

Has anyone seen my chicken?

Lee let everyone see in turn, while he found the

blackboard that had told Hester where to find the rifle. There was chalk in the holder, so he started putting up a message of their own. It read:

Who are you? What do you want?

He pulled the blackboard to the edge of the roof. He took the binoculars from Cozzie, who was still puzzling over the chicken comment, and watched the man read their message, before turning away himself to write a new one:

Just a friend. Are you well?

Lee replied:

All well. What's happening with the world?

The man on the roof wrote:

World still screwed.

Bringing down the binoculars after her latest view, Claudia said, 'Fucking hell, Lee. Ask him something important.'
'What do you suggest?'
'Well, I don't know.'

Lee wrote:

How are England doing in the European

Championships?

The reply:

They got there on time

Lee:

Score?

Reply:

2-1

Lee:

You're a funny man. How's the plague going?

Reply:

All hope is lost.

They all gave up on the communications game and found their seats.

'What's the point of that?' asked Cozzie.

'Maybe he's a security guard, or something,' said Lee. 'I'll try him again tomorrow.'

Leila had sat down on the cushion between his legs. Actually, he no longer cared anything about the outside world.

GB Hope

SIXTEEN

Will began to seriously annoy people. It wasn't so much his constant playing of sport throughout the day, or his manic cycling about the mall, it was more down to his bad attitude. Emboldened by the total lack of any kind of authority, he started being disrespectful to the women – they were like the female teachers he had had at school, Beverley especially – moaning busybodies. Tony monitored the situation, ready to protect his wife but unwilling to tackle such a young boy. Henry was less conciliatory when Will used his toothpaste without permission. He was ready to throttle the lad until Claudia talked him out of it.

Will found an ally in Hester. The young man had seriously offended the normally placid Madesio by moving the white-board near to the American's bed which carried all his family photos, and Madesio was looking to punch his lights out. Hester intervened, said he would sort Will out. He talked Will into apologising, telling him he was going to be a big man one day, but why cause trouble when he couldn't get away from it at the moment. Just be cool, bide your time. Will thought it made sense. He found he respected Hester, who reminded him in some ways of the heavies on his estate in Clapham. It was better to be on his side than not be.

Nevertheless, it was thought best that Will move out of the Homeware store. Hester set him up in a Cookie shop without cookies, down the way from Ann Summers.

Somewhere around the five week stage, Beverley took to her bed feeling poorly. It was nothing serious, she told Dr Afridi all about her long-standing thyroid problems which flared up two or three times a year. Once she had rested for a few days she would be her old self again. Tony was very good, looking after all her needs, taking her meals to their room, keeping the others all informed on how she was feeling.

It did, however, give him more time to be one of the group in his own right. He had a beer with a few of the people, sat talking to others late into the night when Beverley was asleep. In particular, he found conversation with Cathy very stimulating. If he wasn't English, he would have liked to have been an American, and everything about that country interested him, from the Hollywood movies to the food. Cathy interested him. Of course, his wife was still an attractive woman, but Cathy was different, Cathy was extremely classy.

From her side of things, Cathy quite liked Tony. He was one of the men she imagined to have noticed her in there. He didn't thrill her the way her ex had once done, but he didn't bore her either. She thought him a good man. And he was from Yorkshire, her spiritual home.

Neither Cathy nor Tony had given serious thought to the level their friendship should reach. But Hester had, apparently. Finding a moment alone with Tony, he extolled Cathy's virtues, saying how pretty and ladylike she was, not uncouth like one or two American women he knew personally over there.

'You go to America?' asked Tony.

'I have a place in New York. Not on Park Avenue or anything. Tony, you're always welcome to come and stay when I'm over there. In fact, you could stay there when I'm not even in the US. Are we not buddies now? We've experienced this together, haven't we?'

Tony thanked him for the offer. It had not been said aloud, but the mention of New York had been made with Cathy in mind.

Even Cozzie and Leila had a fall-out. During a jogging session with Lee, Leila joked to Cozzie in passing, something on the lines of, why didn't she get rid of those chavving flip-flops she always wore. Apparently they were a gift from Cozzie's mother and little white girl should watch her mouth. Lee had dragged Leila onwards, as Cozzie took up a hands on hips, toe-tapping, don't give me shit or I'll give you what for, girl, pose.

Cozzie arrived at Base Camp just in time to catch the end of Hester and Tony's New York conversation. After Tony had departed, she said, 'Is everyone invited to New York, then?'

'Cozzie, you're invited especially.'

She sat down. 'I suppose it would be nice. London's gone to pot. No work, no money. New York, eh? Not that I could afford to get over there.'

'Listen, you'll have my number, if you decide to go over, just call. Don't worry about trivial things like airline tickets.'

'Hester, where've you been all my life? I dated a footballer once, you know, only a Charlton Athletic player, but you wouldn't believe it, he was the only tight-fisted professional footballer in the whole of London. That's just my luck.'

During Leila and Lee's latest jogging session, she had pointed out a pizza chain which she remembered her brother taking her to when he was last in England. It seemed to have escaped the attentions of everyone else so far. Lee said he would check it out in the afternoon and take her there for her evening meal, if she liked.

'What, like on a date?' she asked.

'Yeah, I suppose, like on a date.'

'I'd like that.'

Lee visited the restaurant later on in the day and left a variety of dishes prepped up in the fridges, before getting himself ready. Clothes-wise at the moment, he was on to a Top Man phase with grey marl smart shirt and black trousers, with new brogues taken out of Schuh. Giving Leila more time, he chatted with Cathy and Madesio, before strolling over to Lipsy, calling her name as he went in. She was not there. Suddenly very hungry, and still to put things in the ovens, he went into the bathroom shop they shared for ablutions.

He was whistling an *Adele* tune, but still she didn't hear him come in. She was there, showering in the show-shower which didn't have a curtain. Lee stopped dead in his tracks.

She was not quite turned fully with her back to him. First he saw the raven black hair wet down onto her sleek back. Then her small, beautiful bottom, slightly lighter in tone than the rest of her, and the fabulous legs. There was just a hint of curve from her left breast.

Fairly blown-away by the image, Lee retraced his steps and composed himself. He then called from the doorway, 'Leila, are you in here?'

'Yeah! I'll be out in a minute.'

'I'm ready. I'll wait in Thorntons for you. No need to rush!'

'Okay!'

When she found him twenty minutes later, he stood up and checked out the floral midi dress she was wearing, making sure to compliment her on it.

'Thank you, it's lovely, isn't it,' she said. 'And look at my new ankle boots.'

He made a big show of bending to take in her brown leather boots. 'Very nice. Are you hungry?'

'Yeah, I am, now you mention it. Are we walking?'

'No, we're getting the bus.'

She giggled, linked his arm and they headed off on their first date.

During their meal he realised that questioning her about her family was a non starter, which was good because he didn't particularly want to talk about his, or about Rachel, for that matter. Instead, they talked about things in general, and about their stay in the mall so far. She said she thought Cozzie was very selfish, that Tony kept looking funnily at

Cathy, and that Hester was doing the same to her. Lee blinked to take the image of Leila in the shower out of his head.

'Has Hester said anything nasty to you?' he asked her.

'No.'

'Are you getting cabin fever? You'll be saying Madesio fancies Will next.'

'Oh, he almost hit him again before. Will likes winding people up.'

'You just stay out of it.'

'Oh, I'm all right. You and me, down our blade.'

'You and me against the world.' Lee looked about them at all the other tables sitting empty. 'Isn't this really weird.'

'I like it like this. I saw a film once where there were only two people left in a restaurant. The waiters wanted them to leave. They went back to her flat, in Paris, I think, and... you know.'

Lee saw her in the shower again. 'Shall we have coffee on the roof after this?'

'You just want to send messages to your new friend.'

'There's something I want to tell him about you. That we had a lovely meal. Finish your wine. It's not cheap, that stuff.'

She giggled and sipped the red wine.

'Lee, we won't lose touch, will we?'

'No, I'll stay near you, up there.'

She laughed. 'I mean when we get out.'

'No, I definitely want to keep in touch with you. We'll both be loaded, anyway, shall we go on holiday somewhere?'

That excited her. 'Where? You decide.'

'We could go on a cruise, but not get off at any of the ports.' They both laughed. 'We could say we're institutionalised. No, we'll go somewhere hot. Somewhere in the Mediterranean.'

'That sounds lovely. You're on.'

Thinking about the shower, but managing not to visualise it, he leant across the table to kiss her.

GB Hope

SEVENTEEN

Claudia and Cathy were up on the roof, talking animatedly on the topic of genealogy. They were in their sunbathing places, but it was too overcast to remove their outer clothing. They drank tea as they discussed how they had traced their families back, and how they both faced a brick wall in the mid-1800s where a key person had simply fallen off the face of the earth. Yes, maddeningly frustrating, they agreed, but what could be done about it if they simply weren't on the census after a certain year, they didn't appear on a death certificate or any other form of certificate for family members?

'Do you think your missing person was murdered?' asked Claudia. 'I think mine was, with the common-law husband being the main suspect. Either that or she ran off to Ireland with a new fella, because we have links to over there.'

'Tough to find her in Ireland, at that time,' said Cathy.

Lee was listening to all this guff as he stood at the edge of the roof, waiting for the stranger outside the wall to decide to communicate again. He looked back at the two women. Right, if they weren't going to strip off, then he might as well go down for lunch. A noise across the car-park made him turn back. It was the fence making the racket, just under the line of sight to his friend's roof. A car was bashing at a padlocked gate to get in to the complex.

'Girls!' he called to them. 'Check this out.' They got up and joined him. 'Looks like we've got locals coming in to vandalise the place.'

Cathy was quite alarmed. 'Well, surely we've got security around the perimeter? They can't just let thugs in.'

On the fourth attempt the car, an old Jaguar, broke through and accelerated across the car-park. Although concerned, Lee did notice that the gate was immediately pulled closed again by two men, so it was all part of the game. The Jag crashed through two zombies on its mad, swerving way towards the mall, making the machines cartwheel through the air and crash horribly to the ground.

'I'm going to run down,' Lee told them.

'Get Henry and Hester,' Claudia told him.

Lee ran through along the cold top floor of the North Blade, down an escalator, into Base Camp. He didn't have to explain any more than a car had broken through the fence because everybody heard it then smash into one of the outer plate glass windows.

Claudia needn't have named Hester and Henry, because they were the two who were at the vanguard of the move towards the noise. Lee played just behind the two strikers, with the midfield of Tony and Beverley, her health improved, and Will and Dr Afridi following on behind. The store taking the brunt of the assault was River Island. Moving quickly to the far wall, Lee could see the smashed window from far off. Hester and Henry were shouting. Lee came through the racks of clothes, seeing the front wheels of the Jag up on the window sill. Shattered glass lay everywhere.

'What the fuck are you doing?' Henry was shouting to someone outside.

Lee got there and looked out. He expected to see a couple of local chavs, but instead he vaguely recognised the man who had been left behind at the London hotel. There was a badly dressed woman with him, and they were trying to climb through the hole in the window.

'Those things are coming!' screamed the woman in a heavily eastern European accent. 'They're going to get us!'

Bizarrely, the thought flashed through Lee's mind that the woman had clearly never watched professional wrestling before. Nevertheless, the zombies were following the disturbance, and he knew they could be a nuisance if they got hold of you.

'Help them in!' shouted Beverley.

The hysterical woman and Alexandru climbed through the damage with the help of Hester. Alexandru was profuse with his thanks.

'What are you doing, man?' asked Hester.

'They told us it was the only way in. The only way for the money.'

Suddenly it became remarkably scary as a dozen or so zombies began scrabbling at the window. Alexandru's lady friend cried out again, and Beverley decided they should remove themselves. Dr Afridi led the Romanians away.

'We can't let them come in!' shouted Henry.

Beverley put a hand over her mouth with shock as she

saw the developing problem. Henry grabbed a clothes rack and attempted to beat the zombie machines back, as the hole in the glass grew larger with every second. Tony and Lee grabbed chairs to assist Henry.

Cozzie and Cathy arrived to see what was going on.

'Mother of God!' screamed Cozzie, which didn't help the situation at all. She instantly became hysterical at the shocking sight which faced her. Leila came in and slapped Cozzie right across the face. Lee, in his frantic pushing with the chair against the strong machines, had happened to glance back at the exact time and saw the blow land. What a girl!

Then Hester fired the rifle, which he had fetched from the post box, five times in quick succession, clearing the window of most of the zombies. The shock and awe of his actions scared everyone numb, then Cozzie screamed again and everyone turned to stare at Hester. Beverley was incandescent with rage at what had just happened.

'What are you doing with a gun!?' she screamed into Hester's face. 'There's not supposed to be a gun!'

Tony held his wife, equally shocked, even though he knew of the weapon's existence. Hester was sweating on his big forehead, but otherwise in control of himself.

'That may give us some time,' he said. 'We need to secure this store.' Beverley was still at him. 'Beverley, this rifle will be locked away and you can have the key. We'll talk about it after this problem has been dealt with!'

Beverley led the females out of River Island, although Leila was reluctant to leave Lee. The men retired away from the windows to examine the entrance to the store. There were two large passageways, either side of a large stone pillar, with the grilles locked up in the open position.

'Probably opened and closed from a central location,' suggested Tony.

'No,' said Hester, shaking his head. 'Every store must have its own way of opening up.'

He and Lee looked frantically around the shop foyer. Will spotted the slot for an allen key in the centre pillar.

'Here!' he shouted. 'Look.'

'Find the keys,' ordered Hester. 'Is there an office?'

Lee ran over to a room to the left of the entranceway. He found it unlocked, so started rummaging around the desk and a filing cabinet. Henry joined him, immediately seeing the box on the wall. That was locked, though.

'Hester!' shouted Lee.

More gunshots rang out – zombies were in the shop. Hester hurriedly joined them, clearly enjoying himself. He took a moment to catch his breath.

'They're not that dangerous,' Hester told them. 'But we can't have them grabbing hold of the women.'

'They're fucking dangerous enough for me,' said Henry. 'Shoot that box open.'

Hester did it in two. Lee found heavy keys inside, one of which fitted the lock when they ran from the store. The grilles kicked into life and descended, just as half a dozen zombies crossed the store to stand rattling the metal.

All the men had sweat soaking their faces and shirts.

'Fucking hell!' said Henry, smiling. 'I wasn't born for this shit, you know. Hey, people, we battled the zombies. Well done, lads.'

The tension left them with laughter and back slapping. Still, they wanted to move away from the manic machines at the grilles.

Dr Afridi treated the latecomers for a few glass cuts to their arms. As the rest of the men returned into Base Camp, Alexandru piped up, cheerfully, 'I'm Alex, from the hotel. Remember me?' He had clearly already said the same to the others.

Cozzie went to Hester, her man in a crisis. 'Are we safe now?'

'We certainly are. All locked down.'

'I'm Alex,' the man said again, in a pleading tone, as Henry had him by the throat.

'What's the fucking game?' Henry demanded of him.

Lee and Tony encouraged Henry to put the man down.

'That was the only way we could come in,' said Alex. 'Drive like madman, they said, and break in.'

'And who's this?' asked Hester, of the woman alongside Alex.

'This is my sister, Nadia.'

Lee sat himself down, happy to have Leila close by, looking at him. He started laughing at the way Alex and Nadia had joined them. 'It's good,' he said. 'If you think about it, it's bloody good.'

There came a general acceptance that he had a point – it was a big game, after all. Only Henry was still to mellow. 'Send 'em down to fucking Scholesy!' he cried.

EIGHTEEN

Hester had cleaned the rifle and locked it back in the post box. Beverley had been handed the key and put it round her neck on a chain.

That made things better, but there was still an air of tension and anxiety, which had changed the state of play in there. The gun had been talked about all the previous evening. Finally, they agreed that if it was never brought out again during their remaining time, then they could all move forward. The topic was left alone from then on, although Hester remained a figurehead for force, and Beverley was one for peace – some of them looked at the man in a new light, especially Henry and Dr Afridi. Cozzie and Will were with Hester all along; Cathy and Claudia leaning towards Beverley. The rest stayed neutral, seeing no reason to make a fuss – Hester had led the fight against the zombie incursion, after all, but they weren't keen on seeing a rifle.

In true British tradition, Alex and Nadia were housed and clothed. To Leila's mild chagrin, they took over Waterstones – Nadia upstairs and Alex in Leila's old alcove downstairs. He didn't seem to mind the rancid carpet. Over brunch in Base Camp, he told them about being arrested in the London hotel for simply being in a staff area, which was code for petty pilfering. Lee smiled ruefully over his coffee, thinking Alex a total moron – £100,000 on offer and he went on the rob. Apparently, he had been snaffled up by immigration over his expired visa, and only freed by a team of lawyers and that man Nigel Gee. So, here he was at last.

If she hadn't made a fuss climbing through the shattered window, they would have thought Nadia was deaf and dumb. She sat there po-faced near her brother, watching everyone with distrust.

Lee leant over to Leila and whispered, 'Glad she could make it.'

Leila laughed. 'Are we jogging today?'

'I don't know. I'm all sore from fighting zombies, you know.'

'You poor baby. We could take it easy and then I'll give you a rub-down in Lipsy.'

Christ, thought Lee. Matters had to be brought to a head soon. He tried to pin down exactly what his problem was – he'd slept with Rachel within six hours of knowing her. He came to the conclusion that it must be Leila's age that was bothering him.

'What are you thinking about?' she asked.

'You.'

'And why not?'

'What are we going to do with you?'

'Anything you want.'

Hester passed by; clearly he must have heard the exchange. 'All right, campers? Never a dull moment in here.'

Lee acknowledged him, then took Leila's hand. 'Come on,

we'll decide what to do over in your gaff.'

Alex fitted right in as a friendly, cheerful, team player. Nadia did not. Over the next couple of days, people quickly stopped talking to her because they hardly got a reply. Although quite pretty, she made no attempt with her appearance, and came across as sulky and shady. She never sat with the group; they just saw her moving about in the colourful, all-encompassing clothing and black head scarf she chose to wear.

Things went crazy within a week of her being there, when everyone but Hester and Will complained that they were missing personal items – two expensive watches, a bracelet that had belonged to Leila's mother, sunglasses not from the mall, etc, etc. Claudia challenged Nadia because she had seen her from a distance coming out of Bedlington's, despite being told it was out of bounds. Nadia reacted as if she had been stopped by the police, protesting her innocence in her native tongue and trying to move away from Claudia. When she couldn't escape the Yorkshire woman, she collapsed in a heap as if having a heart attack. Hester, Henry and Leila were near enough to run to the scene, to see Claudia stripping items out of Nadia's skirts.

No longer seeing the need to feign illness, Nadia got to her feet and brazenly faced them up.

'Why take our things, you crazy bitch?' asked Claudia. 'You've got half a billion quids worth of stuff in here to go at.' She turned to Henry. 'Can you believe this slag?'

Henry comforted Claudia. 'I said she was bad news from the moment she got here.'

Leila found her mother's bracelet on the floor and reclaimed it. Without further ado, she gave Nadia a punch to the face using both fists at the same time, an astonishing pincer movement from someone so slight. As would be expected, Nadia's top lip split right down the middle and blood spurted to the floor. Also, she was extremely shocked by the blow and began moaning.

Leila didn't hang around to discuss the matter further.

Lee was up on the roof when he was told of Leila's fight. He had been exchanging playful messages with his friend in the outside world, but not really getting anywhere. Perhaps he would only get a reaction if he said someone was dead in there.

It was Cathy who mentioned Leila as she came outside, with Tony in tow as her new sunbathing buddy. Lee left them to it and went in search of Leila. She was not to be found in any of the regular places, and everyone he asked shook their heads and said they hadn't seen her.

Thinking Leila would show up when she was good and ready, he joined Beverley and Claudia, who were lunching in Base Camp. He failed to mention where he knew Tony to be, just sat there with some cheese and crackers and a coffee, listening to them discuss Nadia. Personally, Lee believed he had lost his torch to the thief but was not bothered in the slightest.

Hester joined the little chat. It was quickly decided that Alex and Nadia would go the way of Andrew Scholes. Lee hadn't thought of the man for a few weeks. How would he feel if he was banished to live in isolation? Lee asked Hester if he had seen Leila.

'No, my friend,' said Hester, standing. 'Right, what do I fancy to eat?' He went on his way.

In fact, Hester had seen Leila enter the unused cinema fifteen minutes earlier. He thought he would give the little minx a little time to cool off after launching her fabulous assault on Nadia.

Hester entered the darkened theatre. Leila wasn't to be found in the back row, disappointingly. He found her down near the front. When he asked if he could sit down, her eyes flashed up at him, but she didn't say anything.

'Leila, are you all right? Listen, Alex and Nadia are going to move down near Mr Scholes. You won't have to see her again. Do you understand?'

There was an imperceptible nod, where tears dropped onto her cheeks. He sighed, made himself more comfortable.

'You know, Leila. I felt a lot of anger coming out of you when you hit Nadia. Life's been horrible to you, hasn't it? But it doesn't have to be that way, you know. I can help to make it better.' She was crying openly by then. He placed his right hand on her left cheek and turned her face slightly towards him. 'If you trust me, I promise to make all your problems go away. I'm setting up a new place for people to live, with their families, in America. You're welcome to join us. You'd have nothing to worry about. What do you say?'

'I don't know.'

'Of course, I'm just bringing up the subject. Plenty of time for the idea to sink in. Leila, you're so cute. You're adorable.'

'Thank you.'

'You'll make the right decision in the end, I'm sure.'

They sat there for a moment looking into the darkness towards where the screen was. She sensed him turn towards her. Next thing she knew he was opening the buttons of her new blouse. Then he slipped his hand inside her bra and cupped her left breast. She accepted it – it was not a completely novel experience. He took her right hand and placed it on his groin, as he pulled her head forward and made her kiss him. She was extremely unhappy and disturbed by this development, but didn't know what to do. All her feistiness seemed to have deserted her.

It felt like being smothered by a big bear, her blouse fully open, being roughly fondled. Then he made her do what the boys in Blackpool were always nagging her to do. That chore lasted fifteen minutes or so, then she was relieved of her skirt and knickers and lifted on to him without the slightest effort on his part.

After another awful quarter of an hour she found herself abandoned back in her seat to continue her crying.

Lee didn't find Leila until the early evening. He jogged over to her and she allowed him to pick her up in a relieved hug.

'I've been worried,' he told her. 'Are you all right, you scrapper, you?'

'Did you just call me a slapper?'

He laughed. 'Scrapper! I called you a scrapper. Where are you off to?'

She pointed to Lipsy, then took his hand and led him into the shop.

'I preferred your old pad,' he teased, as they wound their way through the clothes racks.

Her den was behind the till area – her Marilyn Monroe and Noel Gallagher prints propped against the wall, along with a new edition, in a homage to May 13th and all that, the footballer Sergio Aguero pictured in full flow for Manchester City. She had a couple of lamps and a clock radio and several books from Waterstones, including the Harry Potter.

She sat on the bed and quickly whipped her dress off over her head, revealing her body to him, naked except for her knickers. She looked up at him.

'Leila,' he said, softly, 'is this what you really want?'

She pulled him forward by his belt, yanked his jeans open and proceeded to perform enthusiastic oral sex on him. As it was happening, he looked to the left and right, at the clothes and mannequins of the store which should have been crammed with shoppers. It was another of those surreal moments for him.

He laid her gently down to return the compliment, then they got under the covers and he made love to her with all the tenderness he possessed.

GB Hope

NINETEEN

Scholes had changed his darts technique from that of Simon "The Wizard" Whitlock to that of Phil "The Power" Taylor.

Treble twenty. Single twenty. Single twenty. Treble twenty. Single twenty. Treble twenty. Come on, stage two passed. Feel the dart like the Power. You're the man. Come on. Treble twenty. Smooth! Smooth! Yes. Treble nineteen. Yes. Just put it in there. Just put it in the Double twelve. Just...

'No!!!! Too low, you knob!!'

He threw himself around the floor, doing a kind of break-dancing while screaming his head off. He jumped up, suddenly consumed by a paranoid terror, but when he checked the Double twelve it was definitely not in there!

'No! No! No!'

Down the hallway a little bit, Nadia peeped through the sheets she had put up on the glass frontage of her new home, at the crazy neighbour making a racket again. Shitty, shitty England!

Lee had just finished making love to Leila in his bed in Thorntons. As they lay entwined, her hair annoying his unshaven face, he suddenly started laughing. After forty-eight hours of almost constant sex, she just about had the will to turn her head and look at him.

'When me and Rachel moved into our Liverpool flat, we Christened every room.'

He laughed again, quite tickled by the thought.

'What do you mean?'

'Christened. You know, had sex in. We'll have to do the same.'

She was mortified. 'What, in a giant shopping mall?'

'Oh, yeah.'

He laughed even harder.

She decided to get up. 'I'm hungry.'

He watched her put on her panties, then find a tee-shirt and jeans. He was hungry himself, so made a move.

There was no bread any more, so they had cereal with their coffee in Base Camp. Leila waved at a passing Claudia, heading up the escalator.

Hester sat himself down nearby with his own coffee and bid them good morning. Lee responded cheerfully. Leila just kept staring straight ahead. She hated Hester, but it didn't occur to her that she could move away from the man.

The zombies at the River Island grilles made themselves heard.

'Good batteries in those things,' said Hester.

'Hester,' said Lee. 'What if we got rid of all the outside zombies? Then we could drive the car around.'

Hester replied, looking straight at Leila, 'What I saw of that Jag, it looked like it had leaked all its fluids. It was completely and utterly fucked. If you want a joyride... go to the bungee-jumping machine.'

'Ah, well, never mind,' said Lee, 'Just an idea.'

All the others slowly started to gather with their various breakfasts. Lee noticed it was Cathy, not Beverley, sitting talking to Tony. Madesio chatted with Will, apparently back on speaking terms. Cozzie flip-flopped in and took her place. She gave the impression of hating the place, by then.

A strange noise sounded from somewhere nearby, hard to pin down in the vast atrium.

'The zombies again,' offered Hester.

The noise came again, more like a human shout.

'Maybe Scholes has done his darts trick again,' said Tony.

When the noise came for a third time, they identified Bedlington's store because they were all straining to hear. Lee set off up there, with the rest of the group following close behind. By the time they made it up the escalator, the source of the disturbance emerged from the bed store: Claudia, dishevelled and in quite a distressed state. Henry stumbled after her, looking angry.

Claudia was pointing an accusing finger at Henry. 'This bastard just groped me! He attacked me!'

Henry just swore at her and tried to take hold of her arms, to make her stop accusing him, but she flipped out and he backed off. He looked embarrassed as well as furious.

Lee stepped in. 'Henry, calm down. What's gone on here?'

'This fucking bitch has been teasing me for weeks.'

'Oh, fuck off!' screamed Claudia.

'She has. You've all seen it. Hester, you've certainly seen

it.'

All eyes briefly washed over Hester's impassive face. Claudia swore at Henry again.

'I was just reacting to your signals,' pleaded Henry.

Claudia tried a new signal for him; she spat in his direction. Henry jumped the distance between them and took her by the throat. Lee had to intervene properly, meaning all Henry's fury turned onto him. Henry's red neck was fit to burst, his shoulders tensed to hit Lee, but Lee suddenly put in two quick punches to Henry's face, only slightly less of a pincer movement than Leila's against Nadia, but with far more force. Henry had bloody, facial damage but in his rage he felt nothing. He threw that punch, which Lee avoided. This was all happening in a flash, and was startling to the onlookers. Lee threw a left hook. Then suddenly the two men were on the ground, with Lee choking the life out of Henry with a forearm across his windpipe. Only with analysis later would they all be able to agree that Lee had dropped down to the floor at great speed, taken Henry's legs away, spun round the bigger man and taken him by the neck, while his legs were clamped round his arms and chest.

Henry was turning blue by the time Hester and Tony reacted to force Lee to release him. Lee fell away towards Leila, Claudia and Madesio, while Henry squirmed across the marble into Hester's arms, surrounded by the others. The groups split on those lines, Madesio pushing Lee and the girls away from the scene.

They ended up in McDonald's, upstairs, taking stock of what had just happened.

'That was heavy, dude,' said Madesio. 'We're halfway through this, and the game just turned ugly.'

'Didn't you hear what I said about Henry?' Claudia asked him, angrily.

'I hear you, Claudia. I'm just wondering how we move forward.'

'I don't want to move forward,' said Claudia. 'I want out of here.'

Leila collected bottled water from a fridge and passed them round. She sat on the top of a booth so that she could lean with her arms around Lee's neck. 'How can you leave?'

'I'll get Dr Afridi to call for emergency assistance. Or can't we climb the wall?'

'I noticed the other day,' said Madesio, 'that the razor wire is electrocuted. It killed one of those tall crane birds while I was watching.'

'Well, Dr Afridi, then,' persisted Claudia.

'You might lose all your money,' Lee told her. When she didn't immediately dismiss the money issue out of hand, he continued, 'What exactly did Henry do? I don't doubt your word, Claudia. But is it something you can't put off for a few months? We don't have to live in his pocket, you know. There's plenty of room in here.'

'Well, he didn't rape me, if that's what you mean. He's a goon, a dick you meet occasionally in a club. Maybe he thought he could get heavy with me because we're stuck in here. Maybe someone put him up to it.'

They sat sipping their water.

'Claudia,' continued Lee, 'it's your call. If you want out, we'll get you out.'

She was wavering. Henry had touched her, but it was only like something that had happened before a couple of times in the real world, where she could lash out with her nails and tell her male friends and somebody would get a warning outside a pub or something. She knew she sometimes attracted unwanted attention. In the mall, she was all confused. Could she rely on Lee and this odd American guy? Maybe the rest of the group would keep Henry away from her. Maybe she could see things out and get the much needed cash. She didn't want to go back to working at the surgery and living with her parents. And besides, why should she be the one to lose out?

'He should be kicked out,' she stated.

'That's unlikely to happen,' said Madesio.

'Well, what are the options?'

Lee gave it some thought, fondling one of Leila's ears as he did so. 'We could de-camp elsewhere. Some of the others might come with us – Beverley and Tony, Cathy, Dr Afridi. Leave the rest here. No-one ever said we had to stay together in a big group.'

Claudia stood up. 'Give me a moment to think.'

She moved off. Madesio went to the front of the store to look down into the mall. Leila was kissing Lee's ear.

'You fighter, you,' she said. 'Where did that come from? I've never seen anything like that before.'

'I've always been into mixed martial arts. I grew up with my dad being a famous black belt in Tae Kwon-do. He had schools all over the place where he taught it. Obsessive knob, he was. I've had half a dozen cage fights around the North-West.'

'Cage fights? God, Lee. Did you win any?'

He smiled. 'Lovely Leila. I'm five and one. My last one convinced me I'm not a very good cage fighter.'

'It looked pretty good to me.'

'Thank you.'

Claudia and Madesio came back to their seats.

'I want to see it out,' said Claudia. 'Thank you, Lee. What do you think we should do? I'll listen to your plans.'

'How about we move into Jon Lewis? It's been pretty untouched so far. We'll have access to the roof.'

'Let's go straight away,' said Claudia.

'Listen,' said Madesio. 'I'm fairly on the outside here. I'll go and talk with Cathy, and some others. I'll see how they feel about what happened. Then I'll join you down there.'

'Good man,' said Lee.

'I'll go now,' said Madesio. 'I won't say where you are.'

He got up and left the restaurant.

They stayed where they were for almost an hour. The three of them agreed that there was nothing back at their sleeping places that they couldn't just walk away from. They discussed whether there was anything they should take down there with them, but concluded that the North Blade would hold everything they could want.

When they made their move they didn't see another soul. The pristine, exclusive Jon Lewis store welcomed them to a fresh beginning. They moved deep into the shop and walked up to the living room/bedroom display areas, Lee thinking of barricading the escalators at some later stage, as they went up one of the two. They sat down to re-group their thoughts.

'We've gone up in the world,' said Lee.

'This is nice,' said Leila.

Claudia nodded. As expected, she didn't feel safe. The crazy project had blown up in her face, just like her mother had warned, but she didn't give way to the urge to cry; instead, started talking to Lee. 'Do you think there'll be a problem with the others?'

'I don't see why. Scholes simply got told to go away. Alex and whatsherface got shunted out, as well. They'll just go merrily on down there, leave us up here.'

'What if they don't?'

'Well, they're not axe murderers downstairs. But let's see who comes with Madesio. Then we match our strengths against theirs. I think we'll be very cosy here. We can move things around to make spaces we all want. They've got everything under the sun in here.'

'Top stuff as well,' said Leila. 'My mum always liked coming into Jon Lewis.'

Then she blushed and went quiet. Only Lee guessed what that was about.

TWENTY

Madesio showed up a few hours later, carrying his possessions. Surprisingly, Cathy was not with him, nor Beverley or Tony. There was just Dr Afridi beside him. Lee had been down scouting around. He welcomed them on the ground floor and took them upstairs. Madesio was looked straight to for the information.

'Henry says he's going to keep himself to himself,' began Madesio. 'Perhaps leaving a way for us all to continue to co-exist. Everyone else is sympathetic towards you, Claudia. They're not sure what to do for the best. Maybe they feel it would be a big upheaval to split the group. Of course, they weren't actually present when, well – you know.'

That didn't sound too bad to Lee. He was sitting on a leather sofa with Leila, in the area that seemed most likely to become their new home. He turned to Dr Afridi.

'Are you happier up here with us, Doctor?'

'Most certainly, yes. To be honest with you, Hester offered me a job this morning. My GP career has certain problems at the moment, but I do not like that man. So, thank you for having me.'

Claudia gave him a little round of applause. 'Thanks,

Doc. You're very welcome. I think I'll find a place to call home. Leila, help me out?'

'Sure,' said Leila, jumping up. 'We'll get you settled in.'

The men watched the girls go off. Madesio sat down. 'Hester has called a meeting.'

'About what happened?' asked Lee.

'No,' said Dr Afridi. 'I think he wants to talk on a bigger scale.'

'He's a shady bastard,' said Lee. 'Tonight? Well, Claudia won't go down for any meeting. Shall I represent us? You two stay with the girls. Unless you want to attend?'

Neither of them did.

'Okay, then,' said Lee. 'I'll see what's on his mind.'

The North Blade had two food outlets, but the first night they stayed with the delicacies of the Jon Lewis food hall, with ham and cheese and wine. Leila insisted on going with Lee to the big meeting.

When they arrived in Base Camp they were encircled by everyone except Hester and Henry, all wanting things to be put right. Beverley was especially disturbed and expressed the hope that matters hadn't got too out of hand. Lee thanked them for their concern, but made it clear that his little group would be staying where they were for the time left to them in there.

Cozzie spoke to Lee about her friend, Claudia. 'Tell her I'm thinking about her.'

'Why don't you tell her yourself? Come and join us up there.'

Cathy appeared very upset. Lee just looked at her, to

imply that she should move up there as well.

Tony shook his hand. 'Brilliant work you did earlier. Impressive.'

'Cheers, Tony. What's with this meeting, then?'

'Hester's called it. Got a big announcement, apparently.'

'I can't wait.'

'Where are you, up in Jon Lewis? Do you need anything up there?'

'I think we're good.'

'Shame about what happened. I'm sure it's been blown out of all proportion, but never mind, we all have to get through this somehow.'

'True. There was bound to be some big blow-out at some stage. A load of strangers thrown together like this.'

Hester arrived and offered Lee a handshake which was accepted. Leila ignored the hand that came in her direction. 'Glad you decided to come down. Isn't this silly? But never mind. I've just got something to say, which might put everything into a new light.'

With that, he climbed up on a chair, and seemed surprised that it held his bulk. 'Everyone. Please, everyone. Let me have your attention for a moment. I know I'm a bit bumptious at times. Hear me out, and then you can all form new opinions about me, if you want to.'

They all sat down. Will placed himself behind Hester, as if he had already signed up to the proposition. Lee saw that Henry was not present. He wondered if he was of the same mind as Will.

'Matters are a little strained at the moment,' started Hester. 'That's unfortunate, but what better time to come at you with something bigger than all that nonsense. Give you something to chew over. I'll stop rambling. I'm wealthy. Wealthier than you may have thought. England is dying, as far as I'm concerned. We don't make anything, we don't sell anything, the people are desperate and unhappy. It's, frankly, grim. I'm getting out. I'm setting up in America, in New York State, Cathy's home state, actually. I've bought a large place there. I have people lined up who want to join me, mostly Americans, because their country is stagnating, as well. But there's room for many more. It's a sprawling complex, made up of little hamlets, a commune, if you like. Completely self-sustaining, it produces all its own food and energy. It's my own little heaven on earth. I can give you all the details, if you're at all interested. Not just you, of course, your families are invited too. You're all here because your lives are not exactly wonderful out there. You felt the need to scrabble faster in the rat race. Give yourselves a chance at something new. Well, that's the big speech. I'm here all night, as they say, for follow-on questions.'

Appearing almost slightly embarrassed, he got down off his chair and moved over to where he had a soft drink waiting. Will moved to stand at his side.

Everyone else sat there dumbstruck.

Beverley finally spoke up. 'Are you responsible for us being in here?'

'Somewhat,' answered Hester.

Cozzie crossed her legs, whispered, 'Well, shit.' She'd heard worse propositions in her time.

Lee found that Leila had taken hold of his hand. He looked at her, but she seemed more puzzled than concerned.

He didn't know what to think, himself, never mind what to say, if anything, when Hester looked in his direction. The meeting broke up, people moving slightly away to take in what they had just heard. Lee looked round all their faces. What were they thinking? Were they comparing their current boring lives to ones they would have in Hester's commune?

As for him, he ruled himself out straight away. Hester wouldn't want him, but the man kept looking over, anyway. Leila. That was it – he wanted Leila. Maybe even Claudia, and Madesio, the American with the ready-made clan. Dr Afridi had already turned down a role in the new world.

Hester was definitely staring at Leila, taking his chance to while she was downstairs. Lee knew at this point that the rest of the stay would not be quite the piece of cake he had hoped it would be.

'We're leaving,' he said to Leila. She was pleased with that.

Everyone politely said good night to them. Hester called, 'Give it some thought. Tell the others.'

'Will do,' answered Lee, leading Leila away by the hand.

'Bollocks to all that,' said Leila, as they walked back to Jon Lewis. 'As if anyone will go for that.'

'I think maybe a few might, baby.'

'Can we forget them now?'

'Hopefully we can.'

He took her into a sports shop on the way. He picked up a baseball bat for his American friend, Madesio, and looked about for a weapon for himself. A cricket bat proved too unwieldy. He fancied a golf club but when he handled one he decided it wasn't useful enough – you would have to swing it very accurately to have any effect. He took another baseball bat, but had already thought about the selection of kitchen knives back in Jon Lewis.

Leila carried one of the bats and they knocked them together as they went up the escalator. He was surprised she hadn't said anything about them.

'Come on, let's go and make a den for us.'

'We don't have to Christen it, do we?'

He laughed and held her round the waist. 'Not tonight, if you don't want to.'

The others had been arranging their places to camp out, dragging beds into place and making walls with furniture. Madesio accepted his baseball bat as if it were the most natural thing in the world.

'Just in case,' Lee said to him. 'I don't think anything's going to kick off just yet.'

He told Madesio, Claudia and Dr Afridi about Hester's speech. Claudia summed it up with an expletive. Then he and Leila went off to choose a bed.

TWENTY-ONE

Leila had found the walled-off section of the store dedicated to selling artwork and fancy mirrors, and had their bed set up in there. Lee looked at some of the price tags on the art, and even on the mirrors, and told her, 'You're high maintenance, you are.'

He had to admit, though, that it was the best possible place. He rested his baseball bat against the wall near the bed – in that respect it was like living in Manchester again.

Claudia made her home in the store room behind one of the till areas. Dr Afridi and Madesio bedded down near each other in the sofa section, purposely midway between the two escalators, the only way up to them on the second floor. Madesio, using his years of experience as a hotel worker, stayed awake the first night. Nothing untoward disturbed his vigil.

The following morning, Lee and Madesio made a tour of the North Blade without going anywhere near the central atrium. While they walked about, they discussed the security of their upstairs position and examined the mechanism to lock-down the entranceway. When that proved to be beyond them, they looked for a way to block the escalators. One could be closed permanently with heavy furniture. They just needed something for the other which could be dragged up in the mornings, like a drawbridge.

Madesio expressed a fear that they might all go a bit crazy confined to just one blade, but Lee reminded him that it was still a relatively huge space for five people, and that they did have the roof. If it got a bit claustrophobic for the last few weeks they would just have to grin and bear it.

When they got back, Lee could see that Claudia was more like her old self, laughing with Leila. When he realised they were collecting swimwear to try on in the changing rooms he diverted away, and went to find a coffee.

Leila found him later, reviewing the exercise equipment. If, as Madesio feared, they all became bored, maybe he could encourage them to spend some hours keeping fit.

'Can me and Claudia go sunbathing?' she asked him.

'Of course.'

'We've chosen the newest bikinis.'

'How very nice.'

'Will you be coming up?'

'I might.'

'Good. Bring some cold drinks with you.'

'You cheeky mare.'

She ran off, giggling. Madesio joined him.

'Lee, I know what we can have on the escalator that we're not blocking permanently.'

'Well, it's beat me. Go on.'

'Two of those mini-soccer nets tied together, with pots and pans and things tied to them. We can push them down and pull them back up again.'

'Madesio, that works for me.'

They spent the next hour carrying two goal nets from a sports shop, tying them together and practising lowering and hauling them up on a rope. Then they picked a leather three-piece suite to throw down the escalator they intended to block up. That worked a treat, added to with tables and a few rolled up rugs. At the end of it they were both shattered and sweating heavily. Leaving Madesio to find some things to hang from the nets that would make a lot of noise if they were tampered with in the night, Lee took three cans of coke up to the roof. Leila and Claudia were in the usual sunbathing place, although the sky wasn't that promising. Without intending to, he found himself squatting down between the two scantily-clad beauties to offer them their drinks. From experience, he recognised that they were both in halter neck costumes. He didn't particularly like the loud colours of the fabric but told them they looked wonderful anyway. Irrespective of what they were wearing, they were making him become slightly turned on. He had carnal knowledge of Leila, and that was fantastic enough, but Claudia was totally hot, he could study the tight creases of her abdomen as she bent forward, and noticed a few missed hairs on her great legs from when she last shaved – understandable while in camping conditions.

He thought it best to get up and move away to have a look around. There was no activity on his friend's roof. The zombies continued to weave their merry patterns across the car-park. He looked at the imposing wind turbine above the main dome. He wondered if it ever turned. Maybe it did during the stormy weather they experienced. Anyway, he considered that to be enemy territory now.

'Are we happy, ladies?' he asked, turning back, sure he was respectable in the trouser department.

'Yep,' said Leila.

Claudia sat up fully. She had on the large sixties-style sunglasses again. 'I think we are, aren't we, Leila? It's nice here with just uncles Lee, Madesio and Dr Afridi.' She and Leila squealed with laughter. 'Uncle Dr Afridi. We must find out his full name.'

Lee left them there laughing away to themselves.

In the glass dome beneath the wind turbine, Hester stood watching the trio on the Jon Lewis roof through binoculars. When he had seen enough, he handed the glasses to Will, and looked at Henry. 'Do you think Beverley will have prepared lunch by now, Henry?'

'She should have done.'

'Let's go down and see what delicacies she's come up with, shall we?'

He led the two others out of the dome. As he ducked through the small door, the key to the post box, with the rifle, recently recovered from Beverley, swung on the chain around his neck.

Hester's group had voted to stop scavenging alone for meals and put together a rota for communal cooking. Beverley organised it – Hester and Henry were excused, Will was too incompetent, so it was herself and Tony, Cozzie and Cathy who were to come up with meals. Lunch was Mexican chilli chicken with sour cream and salsa, a cheesy vegetable side dish, but with no tortillas available.

It was still a happy and normal group. Just because there had been a falling out and a split, didn't mean they should become morose. Hester was clearly in charge, but he didn't ask anything of them. Since his speech, he had not mentioned his grandiose plans for America. He would let them come to him in their own time.

Cozzie smiled at Hester, and he sat down beside her. She disliked cooking, but she was happy to cook for him. Although it was a bit rude to mention the evening meal over lunch, she asked what he would like her to prepare for later on. He tapped her thigh and assured her he would delight in whatever she came up with.

'Is that a new outfit?' he asked, feeling the leg again. 'That's quality material, no doubt about it.'

Will sat himself down. In a surly tone he asked Beverley, 'I thought we were having water on the tables?'

Hester glared at him. 'The lady's busy, Will. Go and get a couple of jugs.' Will stood back up. 'Good lad.'

Cathy asked Beverley if she would like some help.

'No thanks, Cathy,' replied Beverley, warmly. 'Everything's ready to serve. Hester, ready?'

'Can't wait, Beverley.'

The two groups proceeded to get through the days without having any contact. Lee and Madesio continued to employ the drawbridge, but no-one ever came near it. The weather turned horrible again, making it a little gloomy all around the mall. Lee hoped it would flood again downstairs but there was no sign of it happening for a second time. Sunbathing went by the wayside, and Lee saw no reason to go on the roof at all. His people lounged around Jon Lewis. Only briefly did they flirt with the running machines. Leila listened to her iPod.

In bed in their art gallery room one night, Leila expressed annoyance that they had not thought to bring any books with them.

'Is that my fault?' he asked, playfully.

'No. I didn't say it was. It's just that I'd like to read, that's all.'

'There are plenty of great books in Jon Lewis.'

'Not fiction books.'

Lee thought she would just have to do without. But during the following day, he saw her sitting around bored, picking at her nails. He mentioned it to Madesio.

'What can you do about it?' asked the American.

'I was thinking of a 2.am. raid on Waterstones.'

'That's a bit off, man.'

'Alex and Nadia were kicked out of there. It's empty. If we're really quiet, nobody will know we've been and gone.'

Madesio was amused. 'It would boost morale in here.'

'Exactly. Are you in?'

'Sure thing. We'll leave the escalator free tonight. The Doc can sit up and wait for us.'

Claudia was approaching them.

'We'll have to tell the girls,' said Lee. 'Leila will know if I make a move in the middle of the night.'

'Tell the girls what?' asked Claudia.

'We're going to hit Waterstones tonight. A secret book raid.'

'Right! Well, be careful. Could you get me a couple of

Jodi Picoult novels?'

Lee and Hester laughed.

'You'll get what we manage to shovel into our bags,' Lee told her.

Leila wasn't happy, telling him not to bother going to such extremes just to help fill her time. He told her he wanted to go anyway, for the buzz. She was up in her dressing gown, alongside Claudia and Dr Afridi, when the two men left.

They were dressed all in black. There had been a joke about blacking their faces but it had come to nothing. With rucksacks on their backs they moved slowly down the upper floor of the North Blade. Lee had his knife tucked into his belt at his back, but Madesio was not tooled up with his baseball bat. They could tell it was raining. It was cold and ghostly, even with the lighting on. Slowly they crept towards the central atrium. They planned to move down the East Blade on the upper level, then come down to the ground where they wouldn't be observed.

It all went swimmingly. They got to one of the East Blade's escalators and descended, turning back on themselves towards Waterstones.

'No sentries,' whispered Madesio.

For the first time, Lee wondered if Madesio was ex-US military. Not that the man exuded any kind of violent threat, just that military service was more prevalent in America, compared to Britain. Madesio led them silently into a darkened Waterstones. Still the carpet squelched. There was clearly no-one sleeping in the alcoves. Lee tapped Madesio and indicated for the man to go right, he went left into where Leila used to reside. Suddenly he wondered where the Harry Potter's would be, before reproaching himself and beginning to pile any books into his bag.

The time spent in the target location was only three minutes, if that. Madesio rejoined him in the shop foyer, looking for the signal to pull out. Lee thought he heard something upstairs. Madesio shook his head vigorously, but Lee wanted to investigate. If it was Hester or Henry, it might be good to know where they were now camped. With measured stealth, Lee made his way up the wide stairway. The carpet was dry and silent. He thought he could hear breathing, the slightest of snores. His eyes raised above the parapet of the upper level. There was a bed in with all the military non-fiction. A large bed. Was fat Hester sleeping in a King-size? Up Lee went further, almost to the top stair. He made out faces in the gloom. It was Tony, he was the source of the snores, lying on his back, with Beverley's dark bob hairstyle alongside him, and Cathy's splayed-out brunette locks to the other pillow.

Lee rejoined Madesio and they silently retraced their steps. They got by the central atrium without being observed, then hurried home to Jon Lewis. The girls were relieved, jumping up to kiss them. Lee enjoyed exchanging Leila's embrace for Claudia's – he would have to go out more often. Dr Afridi was just keen to get himself to bed. He and Madesio lowered the goal nets.

Claudia was invited to Lee and Leila's bedroom to check out the booty. He emptied his bag and they giddily rifled through the books. Lee sat down, grinning. Leila had a carton of fruit juice on her bedside table which he punctured with the straw and started drinking. It was gone half past two in the morning, but the girls were laughing as they found mostly books they wouldn't touch with a barge pole, but then some they found they liked. In the end, they collapsed on the bed together, laughing away.

GB Hope

TWENTY-TWO

It had all happened suddenly for Cathy with Tony and Beverley. A little flirtation with the man had turned into the one clinch, then the second meeting, still nothing heavy going off. Then to being caught in flagrante, so to speak, by Beverley, even though it was nothing serious. The reaction had been surprisingly calm. It transpired that Tony had a brief history of infidelity, and on one occasion the other lady had moved in with them at their B&B in Malton – not so much a guest as a live-in lover. Tony and Beverley were not exactly North Yorkshire's greatest Swingers, but Beverley appeared to have a predisposition towards the idea of a threesome, and one thing led to another – the lack of a blazing row led to a chat, the chat led to a deep discussion, covering everything from Cathy being in a foreign country, to her broken engagement, to their all being confined in such unusual circumstances.

Cathy shared Tony with Beverley, but she didn't share Beverley with Tony. In fact, she tried not to watch when Tony transferred his affection from her to his wife. She knew she would have to stop being such a wimp sooner or later, it would all get intimate and extremely broad-minded very quickly. She would have to be more adventurous while Beverley was watching, she would have to let Beverley have her way with her. But when she returned to America, it would be to the bosom of her family, not to Hester's little set-up, no matter what he said when he found out about their little polygamous arrangement. Maybe it was what he expected of them over there. Cathy decided that she would let things develop with Tony and Beverley, just while she was in the mall, just while everything was off the scope. She was happy to go with the flow.

The flow speeded up the next morning. Showering in Leila's show cubicle, she was joined by Tony and Beverley. She was a little shocked, but Tony paid her great attention first, as planned, before Beverley moved under the water jet, her black hair immediately turning a darker shade. Cathy felt Beverley's lips close on hers and Beverley's hands come up to cup her breasts.

After a moment or two of this, Tony came back into the picture and everyone was kissing everyone else.

Watching from around the bathroom store window, stood Hester and Henry.

'Come on,' said Hester, tapping Henry's chest and leading them away.

'Those horny fuckers,' laughed Henry. 'And they're not the only ones. I tell you, I think I'll have a go at that Cozzie.'

Hester spun round, and in one swift action had Henry pinned up against the marble wall by the throat and by the testicles. 'Do not,' hissed Hester, malevolently, 'cause any more rifts. Do you understand me?'

'Yeah, man! Leave it, will you.'

Hester released him, as Will arrived on his bike.

'Well?' Hester asked the younger man.

'They've got both escalators blocked.'

'I thought they might. That's the public front of house. The staff would've still been able to get up and down the back. But never mind. Our friends may come to see the error of their ways. Breakfast, gentlemen?'

They moved off towards Base Camp. Will, pushing his bike, had something else to say. 'I bumped into Alex and that daft bird he's hanging with. They want to come back to the group. He said he's losing his fucking mind over there. And Scholesy keeps putting the wind up them.'

Hester smiled and nodded.

After his breakfast, Hester walked over to have a word with Alex. He knocked loudly on the window of the store he knew them to be in, but couldn't see inside because of the covers Nadia had put up. While he waited, he strained to see down the hallway, but there was no sign of Scholes – he wasn't planning on inviting the tramp to join the group in Base Camp.

Nadia's dark, haunted eyes looked at him through a gap in her curtains, then she disappeared. Alex rushed out to see Hester, looking unshaven and far less chipper than when he had made his entrance.

'How are you doing?' asked Hester.

'Not happy down here, Mr Hester.'

'Do you think, if the lady there behaved herself, you'd like to join my group?' Hester nodded in unison with Alex's head. 'We find we're down on numbers. You've got to promise she won't upset the others, though.'

'Mr Hester, thank you. Will said you were a good man. Really crap down here! I'll make her watch herself. We'll be good. Promise.'

'Okay, Alex. Come along this afternoon. We'll be waiting for you.'

'Thank you, Mr Hester!'

Alex watched Hester depart, then shouted at his sister to get a move on.

Leila and Claudia took the opportunity of a break in the storm clouds to do some more sunbathing. Lee went up there with them. He looked at his friend's roof outside the compound but there was no action there. Perhaps he was only a security guard, after all, who got bored with exchanging messages, or was told to stop it. Lee wandered to look over the rest of the mall roof. It looked too dangerous and mountainous with air-conditioning units and mini-domed skylights to go off on an expedition, not that he wanted to. He knew they were on the home stretch by then, it would soon be over and he would be that minted man, free to do whatever he wanted for a while. Would that whatever include going back to Rachel in Liverpool? He heard Leila make a joke that Claudia laughed at, and wondered if he would go to London with his new "girlfriend", Leila?

'Are you two taking the piss out of me?' he asked, turning with a smile.

They screamed with laughter. Leila looked guilty. 'Leila?'

'I just said we should ask for a martial arts demonstration. And Claudia said you should do it without your top on.'

'You girls,' he said, with mock offence. 'I can't do it, anyway. Not on this gravel. I work best on the floor.'

'Go on, give us something to entertain us,' teased Claudia.

He thought of his father. The man was a 3rd Dan black belt in Tae Kwon-do, fighting all over the Far East and North America in his younger years, but all he could bring to mind was visions of the crappy dojangs he watched his father training out of in Cheshire. Lee put in a little routine of front kicks and punches, just to keep them happy. The girls cheered.

'What about the top?' shouted Claudia. 'Off! Off! Off!'

Lee moved swiftly back away from them and squatted down out of sight near the edge, watching the zombies. He wondered why he was still worried about things. There was nothing to be paranoid about, nobody could force anyone to move to America. Why would anything unpleasant happen in their last few weeks? Were they not still under the legal guardianship of that Nigel Gee man?

He thought of the Jag buried in the River Island window. Could there be a way to push that back to their side of the complex? Where they could start it up, check it out, and keep it in reserve. Would the other group be aware of them moving the car? Anyway, the zombies would be on them before Hester's crew came out. Unless they could create a diversion. It was something to think about. He went back to the girls, giving them the loud Tae Kwon-do Kiap shout that should accompany all punches. They cracked up laughing at him. He sat down near to them, admiring their bikini bodies once more. He thought of Tony and his little ménage à trois, then started laughing himself.

TWENTY-THREE

Nobody did anything crazy. Madesio heard Lee out over the Jaguar car idea, but didn't much like it, so they decided not to discuss it again. The heavy summer rain set in once more, forcing them to entertain themselves as best they could in Jon Lewis. Board games came to the fore, they read their books and just talked to each other. Lee found he could communicate very easily with Claudia. He considered that a mature twenty-year-old male was on a par with a twenty-six-year old female. They talked on many subjects from music, to former partners, to what they were going to do when they got out of there. She laughed when he told her about his and Leila's cruise ship plans.

'I'd come with you,' said Claudia, 'but I'm sick of the sight of you.'

'Wey-hey! So, what will you do? Go back to York?'

'Of course. I'll move out, though. Look for a new job. If there's any out there. The country's probably bankrupted itself while we've been in here.'

'If you don't mind me saying so, you're quite fit. Try for some modelling work.'

'What, like my good friend, Cozzie? We'll see. You?'

'Oh, I don't know. I'm as lost as when I came in here. I thought I loved Rachel in Liverpool, but I've not missed her at all.'

'Where's your family's base? Manchester?'

'No, my mum and step dad still live in Mobberley, where I grew up. Mobberley's a small village south of Manchester.'

'Move back there?'

He laughed. 'Move back to Mobberley? No. Don't get me wrong, it's a nice place, but pretty posh and boring. I think I'd prefer to stay in here, than go there.'

'Oh, like that, is it?'

'I'll probably end up like that guy Scholes. Only in York.'

'I'll be sure to look out for you. You will have a mangy dog with you?'

Cozzie was already stir crazy, going round smashing expensive television sets because they didn't work and weren't able to connect her with the real world, leaning her head against outside windows when she was on her shopping trips, to see any sign of life beyond the mall. Not that the shopping was any fun any more, it was just a habit that got her away from the others. The others: she disliked all of them, including Hester. She was only friendly to him because the promise remained that he could offer her some kind of better life. Irrespective of his mad plans for America, she had heard him talking finances, and it sounded like he could buy a London premier league football club if he wanted to. She wanted to stab Will in the face, the little shit. Henry was just stupid, playing at being Hester's hired muscle. He'd be dumped as soon as this was over. Then the three freaks with their weird love triangle. It wasn't what she expected. It wasn't what that man talked her into on Battersea Rise. Then she remembered, it all came back to money, and her lack of it. It would soon be over.

Then the foreign cretins were invited back and Cozzie went ballistic, storming off from the moronic group. Hester found her. Well, actually, he sent that little twat on his bike to find where she was laid down on a bench in the place where they first came into the godforsaken place. Then Hester came along and sat down next to her. He picked up her feet and put them back down on his knees – only because of his wealth did she put up with that.

'I'm fucking pissed off,' she said.

'I fully understand.'

'Now those foreign dickheads are coming back.'

'I see.'

'Can't you put an end to all this? It's all your doing?'

'I have no way of contacting those outside, more than anyone else.'

'Can't Dr Afridi call for help, or something?'

'You could ask him.'

'I might just do that. Ask them if I can stay with them, while I'm at it.'

'That's what I came to talk to you about.'

'You just talk all the time, man.'

'We've got a few weeks left, Cozzie. There's no time for niceties anymore. Move in with me. See how it goes. If when the doors open you want to hang around with me, that's great. If not, then that's life.'

'Move in with you? Into Ann Summers?'

'No, we'll get a bigger place.'

Now the game was afoot for Cozzie. 'What would I be?'

'What would you be? I don't know. You'd just be Cozzie. We can't say girlfriend, can we? I'm married.'

They both thought of the word mistress but neither said it out loud.

Hester installed Cozzie into the upper floor of Next. Perhaps because it was the premier store, or because it was so well known, it had been virtually ignored by them all since the first days. Henry and Will took the best bed up there and cleared clothes racks to the side, moving over all the luxurious leather sofas and occasional tables into a large living space. There were staff shower facilities in the back. Cozzie deigned to go up with Hester and cast her eye over it, then told him that she would be very happy there. Refreshed, she picked magazines and books from WH Smith, found some fake flower displays from another store. She loved the carpet best of all. She told Hester about when she worked in a clothes shop just after leaving school and remembered the skanky, chewing-gum-ruined carpet in the place, and here she was now with an almost virgin one she could roll around on. He liked the sound of that.

Alex and Nadia were to be found in a small stationery shop, complete with plain carpet, their single beds split by the heavy-duty photocopiers. She was no happier there than when she had been banished down to the West Blade. Everyone still hated her and she hated them back – she wanted to shiv them all. She kept asking Alex when they would be getting out, so she could pick up her share of the money and take it back home to Hackney.

Cozzie prepared herself for her first night as a mistress. She showered and did her hair and make-up. She thought it appropriate to choose a new dress from within Next. She pretended she was in a flat in Mayfair, that her married lover was a cabinet minister. Perhaps she was even a spy for a foreign power. At the last minute, she remembered something that she felt would be expected.

'Will!' she screamed. 'Get your arse up here?'

He came into Next on his bike, like a cowboy entering a saloon on his horse. Cozzie had no time to chew him out over it.

'Go and find me a bottle of champagne.'

'Champagne?'

'Yes, or wine, at least. And two crystal flutes.'

'Flutes?'

'Posh, thin glasses with stems. Have you never been to a wedding? And get an ice bucket.'

'An ice bucket?'

'With ice in it?'

'Where do I get ice?'

'Scrape it out of a freezer. Off you go.'

Cozzie checked her appearance again, not short of mirrors in there. Will was quicker than she could have hoped. He actually got champagne and flutes, the ice bucket was plastic but did have ice in it.

Hester arrived very soon after. Maybe he had waited for Will to complete his task, but never mind. Cozzie kissed him properly for the first time, pressing the full length of her body up against his.

'Have you had a nice day?' she asked, laughing.

TWENTY FOUR

Following her first night as a mistress, Cozzie sat drinking coffee in Base Camp, feeling very miserable with herself. It had not been at all how she had expected it to be. In fact, she felt used and bruised. Not that she was a shy wallflower or anything – boyfriends had been athletes, general wide-boys from the local area and the odd gangster, none of them known for their sensitivity. Her mind kept returning to Hester's speech about the commune he was building, and that made her feel trapped. Certain cultures flashed through her head, in parts of the Middle East where women were subservient and scared to drive a car or show their faces, or those Mormon types in America who thought six wives was normal. It didn't help her mood that Nadia, ensconced in several layers of yellow and purple fabric, sat nearby, living proof that some women accepted being only second class citizens.

Henry was there as well, simmering at the presence of the Romanians. He glanced up from his soft drink as Beverley and Cathy passed to go food shopping, mulling over the situation that gave that no-mark Tony a fairly pretty wife and a sexy American lover in the same package, while all he had was a reputation for attacking a woman who had since fled the group. He watched Cathy's rear move away across the marble floor. Perhaps he could have her, seeing as he was banned from making a move on Cozzie.

A primeval scream, one of total joy, filled the length and breadth of the shopping mall. The three people sitting in Base Camp reacted to it with a start, Cathy and Beverley paused on their travels, all those still in bed but lying awake listened to it. Up in Jon Lewis, Lee and Claudia stopped their conversation as it filtered up to them.

'Apparently,' said Lee, 'Scholesy has completed his darts challenge.'

'Another head case. A bit like I'm becoming. Have you any idea how long we've got left in here?'

'No, ask me one on literature. Dr Afridi thinks he's got a record of the days.'

'The first thing I'm going to do, is go into a shop and buy something. Some moisturiser or a Cornish pasty.'

He laughed. 'Make sure you rub the right one on your face.'

'What are you going to do?'

'I might commit a crime. Get myself nicked. I'll pinch a Cornish pasty and run down the street with it. Can't be long now, surely?'

'Talking about crimes, I've not updated my phone yet, as I said I would. Do you think I could still get down there to pick one?'

'Sure. We've had no trouble from the other crew. I'll go with you later. Maybe I should do some more shopping, myself. Even when rich people are staying somewhere on expenses, they still nick the bathrobes.'

'Don't forget Leila. I don't think she's got much in the outside world. And from what she's said, her family will gobble up most of the fee.'

Claudia decided to put on her fairly-new trainers. She turned briefly from him and bent over. He sat there admiring her toned lower back which curved erotically out into wide hips above her jeans.

'Are you and Leila definitely staying together?' she asked, turning back with a flick of her long hair.

'Who knows? I'll make sure she's okay out there, at least. Claudia, you should see a hairdresser when you first get out.'

'Good point. I don't mind you saying so, it has gone a bit feral in here.'

'On second thoughts, I like it that way.'

Claudia was happy with the new phone she picked out, then they went in search of a new coat for Lee. He had entered the mall without one, and it looked certain to be into a gloomy late Autumn when he left. Moving around the shops on their Blade, he was constantly on the look-out for people from the other tribe. He thought he heard the brakes of Will's bike once, but nothing came of it.

She found him an expensive leather jacket. They discussed the pros and cons of wheel-barrowing out phones and coats and all other manner of merchandise when the time came, but decided they would be met on the outside and only allowed to leave with what they were standing up in. He suggested an armful of watches, but she reminded him that the jewellery shops were all locked down.

They could hear another storm battering the roof.

'No more sunbathing for you,' he told her.

'No, back to looking pasty.'

'Let's go up, anyway, and get some fresh air.'

Lee had to force the door out onto their roof area because of the wind, and they stepped into a gale.

'Well, this is bracing,' she said, trying to control her hair.

'Fantastic! I love a good storm. That electricity in the air.'

'Lee, look!'

She was indicating the wind turbine, going quickly round with white flashing blades against the angry grey background.

'Not a total waste of space, then,' he said.

'It's very impressive. I still hate the things, though.'

The wind buffeted them quite strongly. She leant back into him for support and he put his arms around her waist.

'I see what you mean,' she said, breathing deeply, 'about the electricity in the air. It's making me a little high.'

'That might be my animal magnetism. How long do you want to stay out here?'

'By the clock of living in this place, two days should do it.'

He was very happy with that idea.

They finally came down into Jon Lewis. Leila, without any attitude, asked them where they'd been. Claudia showed her the new phone.

'Oh, that's a good one.'

'Hopefully, it will work on the outside.'

Madesio noticed their flushed cheeks. 'Did you run

back?'

Lee and Claudia pretended not to hear him.

'Shall we put the nets down?' Lee asked. 'We're not going out again, are we?'

Madesio helped close off the escalator. Dr Afridi wandered over to them.

'Doctor,' asked Claudia, 'have you been keeping a record of the days?'

'I believe we're into the last three weeks.'

'Thank Christ for that. Do you hear that, Leila? Three weeks.'

The two girls jumped around together.

Smiling, Lee went to throw his new jacket into his den. It was his turn to provide dinner. He sat on the bed to give it some thought. Leila came through and slowly fell into him, forcing him onto his back.

'Three weeks,' she said.

'Aye. What shall we do after it? Head to your place? I assume your mum will be out by now.'

'She should be.'

'It's a shame you've not been able to visit, or at least write. Styal women's prison is up near Wilmslow in Cheshire. Why did she end up there?'

Leila's giddy mood evaporated. She kissed him on the mouth.

'Leila?'

'I'm not from London.'

'That's okay. Why say you were?'

She kept kissing him. 'To impress you, probably.'

'Where are you from, then?'

'Southport, I suppose.'

'I've been to Southport. Good Pleasureland there.' She was still kissing him. 'Good pleasure land here.'

'I've been fostered out in Blackpool.'

'I've been there as well. Threw up after the first ride I went on.'

'I don't expect you to come to Blackpool with me.'

'I don't know, Blackpool through the winter. We could rent a flat and just hibernate. Never get out of bed.'

'You're sex mad.'

'And you're delicious.'

'Seriously, Lee. Are you sure you want to hang with me? I'm not really into being someone's steady girlfriend. I don't mind if you want to walk.'

He wasn't in the mood for anything heavy. He just cuddled her.

'Listen,' he said. 'Let's assume you don't want me to get lost. What have we got in common for when we're living together? What do you like?'

'I like a bit of Speed from time to time.'

He giggled. 'Right, apart from drugs. By the way, I don't mind you doing that stuff a little bit. I'm not into it myself, though. Have you got any hobbies?'

'Besides the Speed? I like music a lot. I want to start going to festivals.'

'I'm sure you'll have a lovely time.'

'I'm also into Line Dancing.'

He laughed. 'You are not! I'd call that a vice, like drugs. We could be a very boring couple, anyway, Leila, so you've nothing to worry about. Do I annoy you in any way? What kind of lads do you normally go for?'

'Blond, or black guys.'

'Breaking the mould with me. I've only got a slightly hairy chest, haven't I? Not too off-putting.'

'Your arse is a bit hairy.'

He hooted with laughter again. 'So it all comes down to whether your guy's got a hairy backside.'

She was giggling and they rocked about on the bed.

'You could have that thing done. The waxing.'

'Waxing!? A sack and crack job!?'

'Yeah!'

He almost smothered her in their hilarity.

GB Hope

TWENTY FIVE

As they prepared that evening's meal inside McDonald's, incorporating ingredients from various food outlets, Beverley and Cathy chatted away to each other.

'I hope the weather brightens up,' said Beverley. 'We don't need another flood.'

'Oh, I don't know. Sloshing around in Wellington boots might just break up the monotony of the situation.'

'Are you getting fed up now, love? It won't be that long.'

'I might go up to the dome, reacquaint myself with where humanity is.'

Beverley kept glancing at Cathy, wanting to touch the beautiful American. She still had the image on her brain of the two of them sharing Tony that morning. Cathy had departed Waterstones immediately afterwards – she was still a little reticent when it came to Beverley herself. Hopefully, that side of the relationship would develop once they were established in America. She puzzled over whether to mention Hester's scheme again. It hadn't gone down too well the previous time. Perhaps, now the shock value had gone.

'Have you given any more thought to Hester's plan?'

'No,' answered Cathy, flashing a look at the other woman.

'Maybe, as it's your home state, you could give it a try. If you don't like it, you could always head to Buffalo, for whatever's there.'

'You mean my family?'

'Well, I was thinking more of your ex-boyfriend. You've said there won't be much chance of that being re-kindled.'

'Beverley, will you really be going? Have you really thought of how life will be?'

'Of course we're going. We haven't got any children. England's a basket case. Hester says it will be cheaper to live over there. He's a very impressive person. I'm happy with him being the leader of the group. Leaders of bigger groups like countries haven't done very well recently, have they?'

'He is very impressive. But, don't you think, a bit controlling? What if he starts telling you how to behave, how to think?'

'Cathy, I've run businesses with Tony for many years and I've dealt stoically with all the stupidity and rudeness of the British public. But underneath, I'm just a woman who doesn't particularly want to be living in this twenty-first century. I would have been much happier two hundred years ago in a rural cottage with my labourer husband, doing what he said.'

'What if Hester said, "you'll visit my bed tonight"?'

'What if he did? I can't say I'd object.'

'Beverley?'

'Don't be shocked, Cathy. Give it a few more years and you won't fancy this way of living any more than me.

Everything comes in cycles. Maybe it's time to go back to little groups of people with a feudal lord.'

'A feudal lord? My goodness, Beverley.'

Claudia asked Lee to take her on another excursion.

'Where to, this time?'

'Boots the chemist.'

'What do you need? I'll nip down for you.'

'I've run out of something. If you know what I mean?'

'Oh, right. Shall we go now?'

He decided not to disturb Leila to tell her they were going out, as she was lying on their bed, reading *A Touch of Frost* by RD Wingfield – not something she would have asked for, but thoroughly entertaining her nonetheless.

He and Claudia strolled down in the direction of Boots. They were comfortable enough with each other not to feel they had to talk. They glanced in a few shops in passing.

'Can we get a waxing product?' he suddenly asked, causing her to laugh.

'Is Leila letting herself go?'

'No, for me. I thought I'd do my shoulders.'

'So that's why you wouldn't take your shirt off. Is it your back completely full?'

'Certainly not. Just a slight fuzziness on the shoulders.'

'I'll find you something. Can I take part in the pulling off?'

'If that kind of thing does it for you.'

They entered Boots. She had a bag with her which she quickly filled with the products she required. She added a box of toothpaste and a small multi-coloured child's toothbrush.'

'Was that for a child?' he asked, entering the aisle. 'How cute.'

She pointed to the pharmacy and photo-shop department. 'We should have taken pictures of this thing.'

'Really?'

'Well, maybe hide them away for fifty years, before any need to reminisce.'

They had moved over there.

'Anything else, while we're here?' he asked. 'Aspirin?'

'Might as well get a few packets of something.'

In the middle of the pharmacy department they came across a large grey metal box, like one of those that telephone engineers used to sit at with a million wires inside. It was slightly ajar, despite having a large MEDICINES – KEEP OUT label on it.

'Is that a drug cabinet?' asked Claudia.

'Open. I told you Dr Afridi is a morphine addict.'

Smiling at him, Claudia opened both doors. Something sprang at her from inside and she fell on her backside with a shocked scream. The zombie lurched forward again, frenzied to have her with big teeth revealed through its lower rotted face, clamping onto her feet. Lee reacted with quick kicks into the thing, while Claudia screamed hysterically. Lee jumped to pull Claudia clear by the shoulders, knowing how it could pin you down, given the chance. In between lunges from the snarling machine, Lee had her away backwards across the shiny floor.

'Get up!' he shouted.

They both backed away, staring at the gruesome

contraption. It was only half a zombie – head and arms and torso, but the rest was just trailing bloody entrails. It came on with remarkable agility, chasing their stumbling retreat from the pharmacy, and then onto the floor of Boots.

'Run!' shouted Lee.

They bolted from the shop and ran back along the concourse, holding hands without actually realising the fact. They stopped and looked back. Claudia embraced Lee with gratitude for saving her. Then they saw the half-zombie propelling itself out of the shop. They ran up the escalator and along towards Jon Lewis. From there they could still hear the thing, but it had been left well behind.

Madesio was near the top of the escalator when they ran up to their base. Lee caught his breath before explaining to the man what was happening. Claudia had fallen into the arms of a concerned Leila. Dr Afridi hurried over. Madesio and Lee quickly dropped the goal nets down the escalator. They could hear the zombie coming, but then the noise became localised on the ground floor, as if it had lost track of them.

'It was a booby trap,' said Lee. 'It's sat there for nearly the whole length of this thing.'

'Where was it?' asked Leila, touching his chest with a gesture of concern.

'In a drugs cabinet. Good job you never went into Boots, with your habit.'

The zombie was still making a racket.

'It's not going to go away,' said Dr Afridi.

Lee looked at Madesio. 'We'll have to deal with it. It's not dangerous, it just won't let go if it gets hold of you.'

They fetched their baseball bats, before hauling up the nets. Claudia wasn't interested, but Leila insisted on going along. They crept down to the ground level, following the noise which was clearly coming from the entranceway.

They found the zombie stuck up against one of the anti-theft radar pillars, slowly grinding the latex from its face.

'What do you think of that, babe?' Lee asked Leila.

'That's minging.'

'Do you really want to watch this?'

'Why not?'

'Okay. Madesio, batter up!'

The two men circled round the rabid machine. They took firm grips on their bats, then moved in to beat the thing to a pulp.

Sweating slightly on his forehead, Lee turned to Leila. 'Did you enjoy that? I bet it reminded you of Blackpool on a Friday night.'

Hester had started to hold court. He told all the people in his group how wonderful his property in upstate New York was – how the little hamlets were designed and how many people were expected to live in each one. There would be all the mod-cons, schools for the children and various entertainments, such as sports centres and swimming pools. Everyone would be designated a job to do, but it would feel like just being a part of the life there. Of course, it was in a remote area, but all the hamlets would be able to interact with each other.

Nadia sat there during one monologue, thinking, 'Here is another darts playing head-case. Shitty, shitty England!'

Cathy looked at Nadia – she disliked the woman, but at least her face reflected sanity. Alex sat next to her concentrating on his food, easy either way, it seemed. Beverley and Tony sat with glowing faces, looking on their leader with adoration. Cathy well knew that to be Beverley's attitude, but she had thought Tony a little more sensible. Will and Henry stood by as brainless lieutenants to their general. Finally she turned to Cozzie, the mistress, and saw that the woman was already looking balefully back at her.

When she felt that it would be okay to move away, when Hester had stopped proselytising, when she felt allowed to get up from the table and leave Base Camp, Cathy went upstairs. She felt ridiculous, a grown woman from the most powerful country in the world, worried like an inmate in a third world country's prison. More than ever she wanted to see the outside world. She looked for the opening to the dome stairs in the back of the crystal feature. Cozzie had followed her up there.

'I thought I'd go and see out,' Cathy told her.

'Like some company?'

'Sure.'

The two women ascended the spiral staircase into the bright dome. There was blue sky all around.

'Weather's cleared,' said Cozzie.

'Still very breezy. When I get out of here I'm going to find out the name of that town. How do you think they'll come for us, when time's up?'

'I hope it's not a coach. Frankly, when I know the money's been transferred, I'll just walk into that town and get a taxi to London.'

'What if you walk into that town and they're all speaking Romanian? That we're twenty miles from Bucharest?'

'Oh, don't even joke about that, Cathy. Don't make me think about those Romanian idiots downstairs.'

'Off to London, then? I thought you were up for Hester's grand project?'

'That's still the plan. I want to see my friends first, though.'

'Cozzie, are you sure you want to do this?'

'What's the alternative? Living in poverty in London as it falls apart there?'

'But to live in a harem in the States.'

'A harem?'

'You don't think you'll be the only one he gives his attentions to, do you?'

At that critical moment they were joined by the man himself, his size dominating the doorway. 'Hiya, girls. Enjoying the view?'

Cathy gathered herself first. 'Yes. It's lovely up here.'

'Well, actually, it's not all that,' said Hester. 'I like to go higher now.' He reached up and pulled down a metal ladder. 'Why don't you come and see?'

'You're all right,' said Cozzie, trying to laugh off the suggestion.

'No, I insist. You can see beyond the town to the motorway. If you're feeling isolated, you can see thousands of people whizzing by in their cars. They're not getting anywhere, but that's beside the point. Come on, Cozzie, come up with me.' Cozzie was guided in front of him, and began to climb the steps, with Hester following, in contact, one step behind. 'Cathy, follow us up. It's really quite spectacular.'

Cozzie reached the roof and Hester helped her push open the hatch. With his hand on her bottom she climbed up on top of the dome. Instantly it felt very windy so she hunkered down. Hester joined her, then reached back down to haul Cathy up.

It wasn't possible to take in and enjoy the view straight away, because the three blades of the wind turbine were in motion, whooshing around some six feet from where they stood, very noisy and each one blocking out the sun in turn.

'Shit! That's scary,' exclaimed Cathy.

She gave serious consideration to how safe her footing was, feeling a touch of vertigo, but sure she had never seen a more secure structure before – it needed to be to support the turbine. There was a small mesh skirting encircling the top of the dome but it didn't make her feel any safer.

'Don't be scared,' Hester said to the two women. He held them both around the waist, pulling them in at the hip. 'Check out that view, ladies.'

It certainly was spectacular, to see beyond the town, to rolling hills and a couple of church spires in the distance. It was unpleasantly disconcerting, to say the least, to be experiencing it in Hester's hands.

TWENTY SIX

In bed together one morning with cups of tea, Lee had found a crossword to do in a magazine, while Leila was writing a letter to her mother, although, of course, she intended to see her in the flesh first.

'Look at us two,' said Lee, 'A right old married couple.' Leila smiled. 'Are you telling your mum all about me?'

'Don't you think she's depressed enough?'

'Very funny.'

'Why don't you write a letter to your mum?'

'No, I'll want to see mummy straight after this. I might write one to my dad, post it in the box downstairs, see if he gets it in a year or two.'

Lee gave Leila's left shoulder a peck, then settled back with his tea, thinking about his real father.

He knew not why, but he found himself back as a thirteen-year-old boy, in a cold Scout hut in the Cheshire village of Lymm. His dad was holding a Tae Kwon-do lesson for about fifteen people, ranging from child yellow belts, with proud mums watching on, up to adult black belts. Lee wasn't participating, instead, sitting with his Uncle Jason on the sidelines. Jason was also a martial artist, but at that particular moment was more interested in the breakfast on his lap. Lee watched his father, in his white dobok with the black belt tied around his rather portly middle. He had big feet as well, in strange black pumps, making him look ever so slightly comical. It wasn't until he started making his moves that he became impressive.

It was the warm-up stage of the lesson, Lee's father leading his students in a jog around the inside wall of the scout hut. Lee lifted his feet off the floor as they passed him, again and again. The students soon started to blow – it was something that had shocked Lee early on in his childhood, how physically exhausting Tae Kwon-do was. You weren't allowed to just turn up, do a few stretches and then start kicking someone in the head. The strict procedures and regimes of the sport were one of the things that kept him from being close with his father, as his friends were with their normal dads.

Round and round the group went. The two out of shape blue belts were sweating profusely and looked ready to collapse. Jason finally took issue with his brother in passing, 'Fucking hell, mate, you're interfering with the enjoyment of my breakfast.'

Leila was also reminiscing. She was back eighteen months or so, travelling in the rear of an embarrassing Skoda Fabia as it came off the motorway at Manchester airport. She could see the WELCOME TO MANCHESTER AIRPORT sign. Where did she want to go? The car took a couple of roundabouts, the Hilton hotel in view, and she found herself travelling parallel with a Metrolink tram, rudely staring-out several Mancs on their way to work.

Her foster parents, Kevin and Dianne, were bickering as usual, that time because she was telling him how to drive, something that always drove him nuts.

'It won't be long now,' said Dianne over her shoulder to Leila.

Leila didn't respond. Instead, she yawned. They travelled along Ringway road. Even a very low Etihad Airways jet coming in to land failed to take her attention. Then they turned right, she noticed, onto Styal Rd – there was a clue. Within a couple of minutes she passed a sign for QUARRY BANK MILL which rang a bell from a recent school lesson. Then up on the left, as they slowed, she made out, through ugly tall trees, the sinister-looking buildings of HM Prison Styal.

Lee was blowing in her ear. 'What do you want?' she asked, pleased not to have to keep thinking about the visit to see her mother.

'What shall we do today? Claudia found an arts shop, says she's going to take up painting. Shall we join her?'

'I can't paint a circle. You can go, if you want.'

'No, no, we'll find something to occupy our time.'

He nudged her.

Perhaps it was that time in the experiment where they all started to think of loved ones, of their outside lives, like captives allowing their minds a little freedom, even if they couldn't follow it. Hester was thinking back, as well, as he sat with his breakfast in a secluded part of Base Camp, behind a combination of palm tree and gold pillar.

He and Nigel Gee had flown up by helicopter to Reading, then been driven out to see the building of the new mall. As they stepped out of the car on a cool spring morning, the pale yellow-brick shopping centre was virtually finished. The car park was still a building site and there were two massive cranes hovering in the background. Being the expected visiting dignitaries, they were welcomed by a trio of excited people in yellow hard hats. Following health and safety madness, they were handed their own hats even before the handshakes and introductions. The architects were a fairly young husband and wife team from a Merseyside firm, wearing his and hers matching leather jackets, jeans and mud-caked boots. The third man was the project manager, a cheery fellow from Yorkshire called Pattinson. He led Hester and Nigel Gee towards a plethora of portacabins.

'Shall we get out of the wind?' asked Pattinson. They stepped into one of the cabins. 'Samantha and Gary have a model in here.'

Hester planted his feet and put his fists on his hips, like Henry the Eighth, and admired the scale model. 'I must have one of these,' he said to Nigel Gee. 'Only bigger.'

'Would you like some tea?' offered Samantha.

Hester ducked his head to look up at the mall. 'Maybe later. Now, Samantha, my secretary told me something yesterday. You're expecting a little one, are you not?'

Samantha blushed and glanced at her smiling husband. 'Oh, I only mentioned it in conversation.'

'Nevertheless, hearty congratulations! I know you only refer to me as that demanding southern bastard, Hester, but my first name's Michael, if it's a boy.'

They all laughed. 'I love that model. But the model's got the turbine on the dome.'

'Within two weeks for that, Mr Hester,' said Gary. 'Perhaps you could come back to see it lifted.'

'I guarantee I'll be here, Gary. Can we have the tour, then?'

'Certainly,' said Pattinson, leading them out.

Up close, the mall looked like giant Lego with blocks missing all around the base. They entered through a makeshift doorway into a concrete space with electricians hard at work.

'Where will this be?' asked Hester.

'This will be Lipsy of London,' answered Samantha, consulting a clipboard. 'Women's fashion and accessories.'

'Samantha, I love your Liverpool accent. I could listen to it all day.'

'Thank you, Mr Hester.'

They walked through onto the concourse, Pattinson attempting to give a running commentary on the progress of work. On the marble hallway it looked like organised chaos, with workmen everywhere and scaffolding in several places.

'A beehive of activity,' said Hester, nodding his satisfaction. 'Lead on, Mr Pattinson. Lead on.'

Cathy had gone for a walk to find a place to be alone for a while, choosing an alcove with a settee in the back of Debenhams. It was not deliberately to do any deep thinking, but Mark, her ex, found her sitting there, anyway. She usually tried to keep him out of her head, and succeeded most of the time, but thoughts of their last holiday together were much too strong and vivid to keep at bay.

Last Fall, they had driven in his Jeep Cherokee all the way from Buffalo to his friend's wedding in Cape Cod. The sheer, adventurous joy they had had of sharing the driving on the long road trip, laughing and talking, stopping at diners along the way. They had forgotten all about their families and their jobs. Nothing else mattered, except each other. She could still remember things he said, plans they discussed. He had been unshaven for the early morning departure and she had caressed his rough chin as they were leaving. She was a nervous driver, but he had trusted her with the familiar, early part of the trip.

She had never been to Massachusetts before, while he had attended college there – those were the friends they were going to. The Jeep developed a mechanical problem just after crossing the state line. Even sitting waiting for help to come was done in a fun way, with Mark keeping her spirits up. They finally got to his friend's house after an exhausting fourteen hours.

Cathy realised she was starting to well up with tears. She resolved to at least contact Mark after all this nonsense. To see how he felt about things. She couldn't wait to get home to America, and remembered the conversation with Madesio in the London hotel, where they said they might want to run to the airport.

TWENTY SEVEN

Madesio had turned forty-three within a few weeks of entering the mall, but had not mentioned it to anybody, just retired to his bed during the day to look at his family photos and open a special letter from his wife.

After that, no celebrations had coincided with the six month internment, until two birthdays came along very near the end. One was Alex, but he kept it to himself, knowing nobody would want to know, and even sister Nadia was unaware of the date. The other was Claudia, turning twenty-seven. They held a party for her in Jon Lewis, with specially defrosted party food, champagne and even a cake that was just about still in date. There were no presents. How could there be presents? – everything was free.

The drinking moved up to the roof in the late afternoon. The rain had moved off. Without hoping for a response, Lee wrote on the blackboard: It's Claudia's birthday. How about a present?

Claudia laughed and gave Lee a kiss on the cheek.

During daytime hours, Lee found himself spending more time in Claudia's company than in Leila's. Or more exactly, acting as her minder, as she was frustrated beyond belief with confinement in Jon Lewis and wanted to meander around the North Blade shops, at least. Her painting phase had lasted precisely two days, when she discovered she didn't really have a talent for it.

They were sitting downstairs in Jon Lewis one morning, looking through the trinkets and underwear she had gathered from her latest sojourn.

'Any more thoughts of what you do after this?' he asked her.

'Not a clue. Unless you're a secret millionaire and need a P.A.'

'Sorry, can't help you there. My uncle's got an engineering firm in Widnes. I could put in a good word for you there.'

'That's much appreciated.'

'Or my cousin lays driveways for a living.'

'Lovely. If I wanted to be a navvy I'd contact my own cousin, down south. He digs up roads for BT. Last year he was working in Wimbledon. Apparently, after every brief bit of sweaty spadework, he wiped his hand in front of his face and a small child ran to him with a towel.'

'Good grief, Claudia, your jokes are a bit on the intellectual side. Listen, I've got another cousin who delivers catalogue parcels. Do you know those films where a Navy Seal team burst into a room and shoot all the bad guys? Then they all shout, "Clear! Clear! Clear!" Well, when my cousin has done his last delivery...'

'No!' laughed Claudia. 'Don't tell me he shouts, "Clear!"'

'No, he does. And he doesn't care if there's people near

him on the street.'

They both rocked on their stools, laughing their heads off. The hilarity fell flat as they realised that Will was watching them from the doorway, astride his bike.

'What the fuck do you want?' Lee asked him.

'Beverley needs the doctor.'

'Right, you've told us. Now go away. Go on, shoo.'

Will took a look at what was left of the half-zombie on the floor before turning his bike and riding away.

Lee and Claudia went upstairs to pass on the message. Dr Afridi immediately reached for his shopping bag of medical supplies.

'Should we ask for a hostage?' asked Lee, in jest, as he received Leila into an embrace. He noticed she was wearing a skimpy blue dress. 'That's nice,' he told her. 'Is it new?'

'Uh, huh.'

'I'll be fine,' said Dr Afridi.

With that, the doctor set out for the other group. Madesio placed himself on a sofa at the top of the escalator to await his return. Lee again thought the American must have a military background.

Lee was led off by Leila. 'What are we doing?'

'I want you to take my new dress off.'

'Do you? Well, if you insist.'

In their art gallery bedsit, Leila knelt on the bed and looked up at him. Lee removed his tee-shirt and threw it aside.

'Leila, babe, you seem a bit serious.'

'No, not really.'

'Nothing on your mind?'

'I just want to have sex.'

'Right, enough small talk, then.'

He moved for the blue dress, her arms raising obligingly above her head. She wore nothing underneath. Lee sat next to her, his interest taken by her completely smooth abdomen. He kissed her neck, shoulder blades and toned upper chest. There was not an ounce of fat on her. He kissed her perfect little breasts.

Normally, Leila was very proactive with their lovemaking – a relative little minx. Lee paused as he realised she was being very reserved.

'Are you all right?' he asked. 'Are you sure you want to?'

'Yeah, this is lovely. Don't stop.'

He pushed on with some of his most romantic work, a little extra aroused because it was daytime and he knew Claudia was milling about the store somewhere. Once he was firmly making love to Leila, beneath him, he saw a tear roll out of her left eye and race down to her ear. That was a first for him. He stopped, mid-thrust.

'No, really, Lee,' she implored him. She locked her ankles around his back. 'Everything's okay. Honestly. Don't stop.'

Dr Afridi wasn't away for long. 'Beverley had a cut to her arm,' he told them all.

'From a zombie?' asked Leila. 'Does that mean she's infected?'

'Good one, Leila,' laughed Lee.

'Apparently,' continued Dr Afridi, 'the Romanians are back in the main group. The woman, Nadia, threw a glass at Beverley during an argument.'

Everyone took in the news.

'Shall I brew up?' asked Claudia.

It was Henry's turn to struggle with thoughts of home, of his wife and of his two sons, in particular, back in Manchester. He had done well up until then not to think too deeply about them, and he knew it was far too late into the proceedings to consider quitting. He sat in Base Camp with a coffee, watching all the others going about doing their regular daytime activities. He hoped nobody would speak to him because he felt completely uncivil. But when Hester did sit down next to him, he held his tongue.

'You look a bit down, Henry,' said Hester.

'Thinking of family, Hester.'

'Oh, you shouldn't do that. Fatal error. Listen, I've thought of something that might cheer you up. Remember when we first got in here? We had to find the electricity cupboard, and we went further on, didn't we, coming across that tram station. Well, I was thinking, why don't we cycle through one of the tunnels to wherever it comes out. Out to civilisation. We could find a pub and have a few pints. You could telephone home.'

Henry sat up straight, no longer the prisoner about to throw himself at the fence to be machine-gunned by the guard in the watch tower. 'I'm up for that.'

'Good, man. Go and dig your bike out. Then we'll have some brunch and discuss what we need to take with us.'

Henry jumped up, clapping his hands together. He set off, then came back. 'Hester, these pints. Have you got any cash? Because I didn't bring any in here.'

'I certainly have, my friend. Drinks are on me.'

Following a light meal, Will gave their bikes the once over. He hadn't been in Hester's initial plan, but was now along for the ride. Henry came back with bottled water and crisps which he dropped into two rucksacks, one going onto his own back, the other Hester's, then they cycled out of Base Camp. None of the others were there to see them go.

In the lower levels, the lighting was still only from the emergency generator. Hester led the way slowly along the staff corridors. He didn't think he went the same way as on the first morning when they were looking for the electrics, but somehow they came out into the tram station.

'Hey, what a cool place!' exclaimed Will.

'There are your scary tunnels, Henry,' said Hester. 'Which way do you want to go?'

'I don't care. I just want to ring my wife.'

Hester leant over his handlebars. 'You're married?'

Henry realised his slip of the tongue. 'Yeah. That's not a problem, is it?'

Hester smiled. 'Not at all. What's the lady called?'

'Tracy. And there's my two sons, Jack and Lucas.'

'Capital, my dear fellow!'

Will was hopping his BMX around, keen to move on.

'Tell me about your family when we get back,' Hester told Henry.

Henry nodded, then pointed, 'Let's go that way.'

'That way it is.'

The three of them headed into the left hand tunnel. The going was unnerving, lit only with the emergency lights overhead, their wheels weaving across the shallow tram tracks. The tunnel seemed very straight. Occasionally, they passed a fire escape cubicle. After about ten minutes of steady cycling, Henry was the first to speak, 'Where's this park and ride station? Birmingham?'

They realised they had been riding round a long bend as a red light ahead broke up the monotony of the trip.

'What's that?' asked Will.

Hester considered ordering the boy forward to investigate, then instead they all slowed their pace and coasted to the red light. The back end of a stationary tram became visible in the half light. There was no space down the sides.

'Fuck,' said Henry, 'Is that the end of that, then? I really wanted to speak to my wife.'

'She might not have been in, anyway,' suggested Will.

'Maybe not,' said Henry.

'Out with her new fella.'

They all laughed. Will was pleased with his little joke. Hester dismounted, gave his bike to Will to hold. The tram had no rear platform, it was a solid aluminium end with a door in the centre, the red light above that. Hester tried the door. When it opened, he stepped up into the carriage. It was even gloomier than the tunnel itself, but clearly empty. Hester looked back to the other two. 'Why don't we cycle to the front, boys?'

Henry laughed hilariously, shocking the other two. 'Sorry. I was remembering an old episode of *Top Gear*, where Jeremy Clarkson took a car into the channel tunnel train. He had to drive along inside it, and asked if he was supposed to drive all the way to France inside the train.'

Hester looked at Henry as if to say "have you finished?" 'Come on, pass the bikes up.'

They regrouped in the carriage. Hester led the way down the long tram, riding slowly, passing across three junctions between carriages, Henry behind, Will bringing up the rear. Before halfway along they became aware of natural light up ahead. The tram was sitting just in the entrance to the tunnel – they were cheered by the realisation.

'Soon be at the pub!' called back Hester.

The other two replied with happy shouts.

'A nice country pub!' said Henry.

Hester pulled them up at the front of the tram, just behind the driver's cab. Sunlight flooded in as he peered about him, seeing an expanse of white gravel and mesh fences on either side of the track. They tried to force open a carriage door but it was hydraulically sealed tight. Henry made a noise of exasperation, so near yet so far. Hester found they could enter the driver's compartment. From there they could get out and down to the track.

'Well done, mate,' called Henry.

Hester went first, reaching back to take down the three bikes in turn. They pushed the bikes out into the sunshine, trying to make sense of their location.

'I presume we carry on cycling,' said Hester. 'We're not at a park and ride station yet.'

They rode up a slight incline away from the tunnel. The nearby town appeared on their left across fields, taking all their excited attention, the three of them all thinking independently of whether to head over that way or keep going on.

If it hadn't been for the noise of loud moaning, they would have ridden straight into the wall of rabid zombie machines, moving forward over the rise with more aggression than the car-park ones. Will squealed louder than his brakes. Henry barged into the rear wheel of Hester's bike.

'Back!' screamed Hester. 'Back!'

They turned about in a panic, Will just getting his legs pumping the pedals before a zombie closed the gap on him. They rode frantically back to the tram, looking left and right as they did so, but the fence hemmed them in. Henry got there first, abandoning his bike and hauling himself up into the driver's cab. Hester and Will tied for second place. As they got into the cab, looking back at the first approaching zombies, they realised that Henry was having trouble with the connecting door to the carriages.

'It locked behind us!' exclaimed Henry.

'The fuck it did!' cried Hester, yanking at the door himself.

The realisation dawned on them that they couldn't return the way they had come. The zombies were almost at them, moving fast.

'Will, close the door!' shouted Hester.

Will did what he was told. Three zombies threw themselves into tremendous head-butts at the tram windscreen, leaving a mixture of fake blood and brains in wide smudges as they fell away. Zombies were up alongside the cab, trying to get to them. Will felt himself buffeted as he kept his back to the door. He was terrified.

'Fuck me!' shouted Hester. 'They're only toys. Let's figure

this out, men.'

Two more zombies came flying into the windscreen, leaving a crack between the streaks of matter. Suddenly they were besieged in the confined space.

'Shit!' shouted Henry. 'What do we do?'

Hester tried to think, with zombie heads smashing into glass on three sides around them. The glass at the side of the cab was weaker. A male zombie came shockingly through and lunged for a screaming Will. Henry jumped across to batter the thing back outside, but it was replaced by several others. Again, zombie heads thumped the main windscreen – it wouldn't hold for ever.

Henry and Will had to fight off another concerted effort to get into the cab. Glass shards flew all around their faces. Hester knew there had to be an answer – it was his game, after all. He looked down at the control panel in front of a single seat. It seemed fairly rudimentary. He sat down, jumped as yet another zombie smashed the windscreen right in front of his face, then hit the big green button. The panel lit up. He had a joystick right in front of him. Will screamed like a little girl as glass cut an arm up to the elbow. Henry was punching malleable faces through the openings to the sides. Hester pulled the joystick gently back, and the tram started to move. Henry laughed involuntarily.

They were heading backwards into the tunnel at a couple of miles per hour. Relief was mixed with further distress as they were taking five zombies with them which were rabidly trying to force entry through the damaged windscreen. Will and Henry rushed to fight them off, one dropped but four were almost in. The noise in the cab was horrendous, moans and rage. In all his panic, Hester realised he was thinking about awarding performance bonuses to the zombie technicians.

Henry at last made his mind work, looking round in the cab for a weapon. He found a small, red metal fire extinguisher which he proceeded to batter into the zombie faces in a frenzy, until all were forced off the tram. Then he slumped down, Will joining him. Both were exhausted.

Hester put the joystick to neutral when he realised the cab was in the open expanse of the mall station and the tram glided to a stop. All three men looked at each other for a moment, before they ran to the safety of the staff quarters.

'That pint will have to wait, I suppose,' said Henry.

GB Hope

TWENTY-EIGHT

A few days later, Claudia and Leila were up on the roof, no longer the time for sunbathing, just there to get out of Jon Lewis for a while and take in some air. Sirens drifted to them on the wind, and at one point a police helicopter crossed the sky – just further reminders that the real world awaited them soon.

Leila finished *A Touch of Frost,* discarded it under her lounger, and looked over at Claudia, who was onto the last magazine in her possession. 'Claudia, do you fancy Lee?'

Claudia was taken by complete surprise. She took her time shutting the magazine. 'Why ask that?'

'Because I think you do. I don't mind, you know.'

'Yeah, Lee's great. I wouldn't try and get between you two, though.'

'You can if you want.'

Claudia sat up straight. 'Leila, please explain what you mean.'

'We're out of here soon. I don't need a boyfriend, and I don't really want Lee to come up to Blackpool. I love him, and everything. But it ain't happenin', if you know what I mean?'

'God, Leila, I'm sorry you feel like that. I'm not interested in him, really.'

Leila suddenly seemed annoyed and offended. 'Why not? He likes you. You'd make a lovely couple.'

Claudia laughed. 'Leila... Couldn't you wait until we get out. I mean, it wouldn't be fair to him, to uproot him again.'

'We could just swap places, you and me. You could have the art gallery.'

Claudia was shocked again. 'With Lee? Just like that? And there was me thinking *I* was a hard-faced bitch.'

They heard footsteps approaching, both grabbing for their reading material, expecting it to be Lee. It was Hester and Henry who stepped out onto the roof – an unpleasant surprise to both girls.

'Good morning!' said Hester, jovially. 'Sorry to disturb you, ladies. This is still a public place, is it not? We've come to shoot zombies. It's a little boring down there in our little group.' Claudia then noticed the rifle, the muzzle being wafted around in their general direction. 'Do you want a go, Claudia? I seem to remember you liked it last time.'

'No, thank you,' said Claudia, through pursed lips.

The rifle levelled on Claudia's face. Hester made a show of fingering the trigger guard. He did, however, aim to the side when he pulled the trigger, which produced a metallic click.

Hester began to load the rifle. Henry was deliberately between the girls and the door to downstairs, not looking at them. Hester moved away from them to take a few token pot shots at the zombies. Once again, he thought, whichever firm that had developed and built the things needed to be given a hefty bonus. When he turned back to the girls, he was pleased that Claudia was on her feet, making it known that she wouldn't be intimidated. It meant that she was further away from Leila, who he stepped over to and bent to whisper down to. 'Leila, it's a great disappointment that you chose to hide yourself away up here. It's not too late to come down and join the others. Variety and all that. I'd take it as a personal favour if you'd consider it. If you don't come down I might think you're being brainwashed into staying here. I might think your friend, Lee, was to blame. You wouldn't want anything to happen to him, now, would you?'

Leila remained impassive until he had finished and was moving away. Claudia stared the two men out as they departed the roof. When she was sure they were completely away downstairs, she grabbed Leila's hand and took her in.

Lee was livid – it took Madesio several minutes to make him calm down, and not go storming into Base Camp. 'Pick your battles,' said Madesio. He judged it was safe to let go of Lee's shirt. 'Let's stay away from those psychos, man.'

'You're right. You're right, of course. Two weeks to go. Two weeks in here.'

He said the last bit for Claudia and Leila, who were sitting quietly on a sofa together.

Dr Afridi, in a nearby armchair, spoke up. 'That Jaguar car.'

'Sorry, Doctor?' asked Lee, still pacing about like a caged tiger.

'We should get the car. As insurance.'

'He's right,' said Madesio. 'Better to have it round here

with us.'

Lee blew out his cheeks, then sat down. 'Okay. Let's talk about it.'

First, they would have to check where they could keep the car, assuming they could retrieve it at all. Secondly, they could not risk turning the engine on to keep it secret from the others. They would have to push it back, and that left the main problem – how to avoid being pursued by the zombies? Claudia volunteered to be a decoy. 'Get me on a bike,' she said. 'I'll ride close to them, lead them off away from the place where the car is.' She waved away their concerns about what would happen if a few of them got hold of her. 'I'll keep my wits about me, stay the right distance between them all.'

'All right,' said Lee. 'Once we're clear, we get to the car. Dr Afridi will steer – you can drive, can't you, Doctor? Yes, good – then me and Madesio will push it back to Jon Lewis. They must have a service bay down there.'

'And me,' said Leila. 'Don't forget me. I'll push as well.'

Lee looked at Leila, knowing better than to deny her permission to go along. 'Madesio, we should go and reconnoitre the staff area of Jon Lewis, and also above River Island.'

'I agree.'

They left immediately, going downstairs, heading through doors marked Staff Only. Along a corridor with storage and rest rooms, they came to a fire exit. They pushed the bar and were out into a large concrete loading bay where lorries would back in. There were a few zombies wandering in view. It all seemed open, apart from a fuel storage area surrounded by wooden fences. Lee ran across to it, found that it opened with a large sliding bar. He gave thumbs up as he ran back to Madesio, and they locked themselves back inside the building.

Next, they headed to the roof, and slowly started winding their way between the air conditioning units towards the central atrium. Lee smiled at Madesio; they were starting to enjoy themselves. Up there, they could not be seen, except from the dome, and that appeared to be unoccupied. They could see the tennis court fence far off on another Blade. When they estimated they were on top of River Island, they slowly went to the edge and peered over. The back half of the Jaguar was visible, standing in a sea of white glass particles.

'You don't think the front is stuck, do you?' asked Lee. Madesio just shrugged. 'Or, what if the tyres are punctured?'

'We won't know until we get there.'

'So, Hester and his people can't see us approach, can they?'

'I don't see how they could.'

They both sat down on the white gravel rooftop.

'Right, we're on, then,' said Lee. 'Let's go and get Claudia a bike.'

'We're doing it now, then?'

'Why not? Do bikes still have bells on?'

They went down to their nearest sports shop and got Claudia a pink Ladies bike. She was less than impressed with it when they presented it to her.

'Who's going to see you?' asked Lee.

She indicated the coloured tassels on the handlebars.

'Tassels, on a woman's bike?'

'We took them off a child's one, actually. To make the zombies chase you more.'

'Shit!'

As with all modern sporting events, they all drank some water before setting off. Lee suggested a team hug but there were no takers. They were in their most practical footwear. Lee checked Claudia over.

'What are you looking at?' she asked him.

'Making sure nothing's hanging off you that could get caught in the wheels. Don't lose concentration.'

'I won't.'

They moved off down the escalator, Lee carrying the bike. Leila was next to him. 'Don't you move away from my side,' he said to her.

'I won't, don't worry.'

Just before they got to the fire exit, Lee stopped them and demanded their serious attention. When they were all looking at him, he said, in true *Hill Street Blues* fashion, 'Let's be careful out there.'

Everyone exhaled and laughed, Claudia and Leila both slapping his arms.

They opened the fire exit. Lee held the bike while Claudia mounted. For a second he thought she looked pretty incompetent on it, but then she rode strongly away from them. The four of them edged along the outside wall of Jon Lewis, watching Claudia ride off between the visible handful of zombies and the main bulk known to be around the corner. She went out of sight for a good sixty seconds.

'Will it work?' mused Madesio.

Then they saw her return, weaving slowly from left to right, heading into the four nearby zombies, but always in control. Then came the bizarre sight of perhaps two dozen zombies staggering after her.

'Good girl,' said Madesio.

'Take 'em far over there,' said Lee.

It was excruciating, waiting on the pace of the lumbering machines. Lee went to the corner. The others watched him look round, then glance to see how far Claudia was getting away, then he waved his arm vehemently. They all joined him at a jog, and continued running along the other side of the building, which was in shade.

They got to the crashed Jaguar, disturbed to find its front wheels up on the shattered window ledge. Immediately, Lee and Madesio jumped up into River Island to start pushing the car backwards, while Dr Afridi kept a good look-out. Lee and Madesio had to rock the bonnet as they heaved on the car, managing to get it to fall back onto the tarmac. Leila excitedly applauded their success, then she screamed at the sudden appearance behind Lee and Madesio of the zombies from inside the store. The two men had to spin round to punch and kick the machines trying to grab them. Then they took their chance to jump clear. The Jaguar still had to be reversed before it could be pushed to Jon Lewis. They opened the doors and hauled it away from the building. Dr Afridi jumped in to the driver's seat, turning the wheel frantically as they other three started to push from behind. On its forward journey the car went near to the window again, allowing two zombies to scrabble out onto the bonnet.

'Keep pushing,' shouted Lee. 'Let's get it away before we

deal with them.'

They pumped their legs, moving the Jaguar back the way they had come. The two zombies on the bonnet were making efforts to get to know Dr Afridi through the broken windshield. He put the wipers on to distract them.

When they were far enough clear of River Island, Lee and Madesio stopped pushing and moved to deal with the zombies. The machines seemed to have locked onto the driver.

'Start the engine!' shouted Lee. Dr Afridi tried the ignition. The engine turned over on the third attempt. Lee and Madesio grabbed the back of a zombie each and dragged them to the floor. 'Reverse!' screamed Lee. Back went Dr Afridi, with Lee and Madesio frantically kicking the zombies. 'Forward!' Dr Afridi engaged first gear and drove on top of the zombies. They were trapped, but still active. It just gave them all a breather. 'Doctor, get out!' shouted Lee. He swapped places with Dr Afridi. 'Madesio, you three go ahead, open the gates. When you're nearly there, I'll drive through these things and get to you.'

'Okay!'

Lee was left alone with the metallic thrashing underneath the Jag. It seemed an age watching the other three run for home. Then he revved the engine, holding it on the handbrake, released and shot clear of the zombies. In his rear view mirror he checked to see if they were left behind, and was delighted to see them both thrashing about like fish out of water.

The Jaguar was corralled and the engine switched off. Lee, Leila, Madesio and Dr Afridi moved to the safety of the fire exit. They all turned round to look – what had happened to Claudia?

GB Hope

TWENTY-NINE

A grinning Claudia made it back safely from her mission, skidding to a stop before letting the bike fall to the ground. She skipped into Lee's arms and was lifted into the building, with Madesio slamming the fire door shut behind them.

'Wow, that was great!' beamed Claudia, panting. 'Can we do it again?'

Lee looked at her as if she were crazy, then laughed with her, continuing to hold her body up against him. Remembering Leila, slightly ahead of them on the corridor, they put each other down, and followed the others back upstairs.

The mood in the camp was one of elation – a good result achieved with no injuries reported. There was champagne left in the fridge from Claudia's birthday party. Lee noticed that Madesio went for a check round the upper level before settling down with his drink.

Claudia described her adventures over the far side of the car-park with the zombies in pursuit, once she almost turned straight into one, then Dr Afridi was encouraged to tell what it was like to have two of the things trying to get at him through the car windshield.

'When it's all calmed down out there,' Madesio said to Lee, 'we'll go and check the car over.'

Lee nodded. He clinked glasses with Leila next to him. 'Well done, you.'

'Thank you. It was nothing really.'

Once the joviality had settled down, Leila moved away from everyone else. Lee found her in the art gallery, collecting up her things.

'Leila, what are you doing?'

'Getting my shit together. Can you help me find somewhere else to sleep?'

'Why are you doing this?'

She moved to him and kissed him as if nothing were amiss at all. 'Don't think me a bitch, Lee. I just want to be alone. I want to leave here the way I came in.'

'But you came in with me. Have I upset you in some way?'

He had a flashback to the way he held Claudia downstairs, not to mention the time he was spending with her in general.

'Of course not,' said Leila. 'It's not you, it's me.' She giggled. 'That's the first time I've said that.'

He gestured for her to sit with him on the bed, and she was happy to be sat down. 'Let's talk about this for a minute, Leila. You can do what you want, of course. Just hear me out. Are we splitting up? I don't want to lose you. You're the loveliest, cutest thing I've ever known in my whole life.'

'Apart from Claudia.'

There it was, but said in such a sweet way again.

'There's nothing between me and Claudia. We're just

mates. I'm sorry if you didn't like it when I had to hold her earlier. Honestly, there's nothing between me and Claudia.'

'Well, there bloody should be, Lee, because you two are perfect for each other!'

'What?'

'You should definitely ask her out.'

Lee rolled his eyes. 'Christ, is this normal for 2016? When did I suddenly get old? Leila...'

'Lee, I don't mind. It's been great fun. I even know what proper lovemaking is like now, thanks to you. We're finished. Do you want me to slap your face?'

'That would be a no.'

'I once punched a lad in Blackpool who wouldn't let me finish with him.'

Lee sat there feeling like he'd been punched.

'Okay,' he finally said. 'You're the boss. We'll still be friends, yeah?'

'Of course. We'll text each other and maybe meet up.'

They embraced for a long time. Then he fixed her up a bed in the far corner, while Madesio, Dr Afridi and Claudia watched on with varying levels of interest.

Claudia told Lee, when they were in bed together one evening in the art gallery, that a 19th century ancestor, by the name of Jackson Grundy, had been widowed in June 1823, but remarried in December 1824.

'Are you still thinking about Leila?' he asked. 'That's been three days. I know it's really bizarre, but she did virtually insist we get together.'

'It's just a little post-coital mumblings, I suppose. In

those days, Jackson, being a farm labourer, would have needed a new wife. No time to be moping around for years.'

'You're comparing me to a farm labourer from the 1820s?'

'No, not really. Jackson went on to have twelve children.'

'Good job he changed wives, then. Maybe he bumped off the first one, because he really fancied the other woman.'

'Don't you be horrible about my ancestors.'

'Claudia... just a minute.' He broke off to play with her tremendous breasts, like a boy with a new toy. 'Where was I? If we stay together after all this, will you do something for me?'

'What more could a girl do for you, Lee?'

'Do some research on my family tree?'

'Oh, that? That's already well into the planning stages.'

They laughed, kissed, snuggled in some more.

'And, Claudia?'

'Yes, Lee?'

'When you get fed up with me, you will find me a new girlfriend, won't you?'

'Shut up.'

Next morning, very early judging by the lack of light coming down through the Jon Lewis skylights, someone knocked on one of the fake wooden walls to the art gallery, making an expensive mirror shake and almost fall.

'What?' asked Lee, grumpily.

It was Madesio. 'That Scholes guy is downstairs.'

'Give me a minute.'

'Okay.'

Lee was actually inside Claudia at the time, her face on the pillow. She turned her head, her damp hair spidery across her forehead, her eyes straining to seek him out in the gloom. She was not best pleased. It took an enormous mental effort for Lee to pull away. He felt her collapse her body to the mattress, as if in protest.

'Sorry,' he said to her right ear. 'I'd forgotten about him. Might be trouble.'

She made a strange humph noise and closed her eyes, making do with sleep. Lee gave himself a moment to compose himself, before getting dressed. He put his knife in his belt at the back of his jeans and went to find Madesio.

The American was at the escalator. The two of them peered over the top of the goal nets, where Scholes could be seen loitering on the ground floor.

'Have you spoken to him?' asked Lee.

'No, I thought I'd better get you first.'

They hauled the nets up, before descending halfway down the escalator. Scholes, as scruffy as always, stopped his shuffling about and looked up at them.

'Yeah, what?' asked Lee

'I want to see the doctor.'

'It's out of hours, fuck off.'

'Don't be like that. I can't stop throwing up.'

'You'd better not be throwing up down there.'

'You're very mouthy, all of a sudden. I want to see the doctor.'

'Are you still at the same place? Well, we'll send him along when he's ready.'

'Very good of you,' said Scholes, with heavy sarcasm.

Lee and Madesio watched him head to the exit. They were joined by a blurry-eyed Dr Afridi, eating from a bowl of cereal. They told him about his new patient. Dr Afridi grunted and sat down. Then, as they were up anyway, Madesio and Lee decided to go down and look over the Jaguar, which they had so far forgotten to look at. Dr Afridi agreed to stay where he was until they got back.

Down through the staff bowels of Jon Lewis, they found their way back to the fire exit. They opened it gently and peeked out, with nothing frightening jumping at them. As it was a windy day, they propped open the door with a fire extinguisher and jogged over to the Jaguar in the fenced area where they had left it. Madesio knew more about cars, so Lee stood guard as the Jag's engine was turned over and Madesio checked under the bonnet. It took a few minutes, Madesio making positive facial expressions as he moved back to Lee's side. Lee was indicating a massive pall of smoke drifting in the sky, a few miles to the south of them. 'Big fire there.'

'Oh, yeah. Nothing to do with us.'

'No.'

They returned to Jon Lewis, allowing Dr Afridi to get dressed and set off on his house visit to Andrew Scholes. They dropped the goal nets after him, and made their own breakfast.

THIRTY

Hester raised the rifle to his right shoulder. He had to aim with great precision as the River Island security grilles had very small gaps in them. He took down three zombies with shots to the head. Expecting there to be more, he rattled the grille to attract them, but to no avail. Perhaps they had wandered back outside, he thought, before returning with a leisurely stroll to Base Camp.

'Henry!' he called. 'Henry!'

Beverley and Tony stood looking at him as he approached them with the rifle. Beverley's arm was still heavily bandaged after being cut by Nadia's flying glass.

'Beverley, how's your arm?' he asked.

'Still hurts like hell, Hester. But can't be helped, I suppose.'

'Make sure you rest it. Have you seen Henry?'

He spotted Henry and walked over to join him, putting a hand on his shoulder.

'What's up, boss?' asked Henry.

'Our Beverley there, her arm slashed to buggery. I think it's time our Romanian guests be asked to leave us.'

'Too right it's time.'

'Where are they?'

'In their gaff, I think.'

'Get Will. We'll have our first evictions.'

Hester sat down and waited patiently for Henry to find Will, then the three of them walked to Waterstones. From outside, they could see clothing, food containers and books flung everywhere, as if Alex and Nadia had deliberately chosen to trash the place. Hester spread his hands at Will and Henry, as if to say "I rest my case." They entered, quickly finding nobody on the ground level. They took the stairs three abreast like Wild West gunslingers. Alex and Nadia's faces turned to see them, from where they sat smoking and eating chips. Alex stood up. Hester stepped up close to the Romanian man's face.

'Alex, we're here to tell you that we all want you to leave. Both of you.'

'What are you saying here?' asked Alex, angry at the intrusion. 'Man, you talk crap. We stay for the money.'

Hester offered Alex a sealed envelope. 'You'll get your money. Give that to the people on the outside and they'll pay you in full. If you're not happy, you can always try to make your way back in.'

'How we expected to leave this place?'

'You take the Jaguar.'

'And if we choose to stay?'

'That's not going to happen. You leave through River Island in fifteen minutes. Whether you go peacefully or not is up to you.'

Alex and Nadia chose to go, but they left uttering threats in their native tongue and with Nadia doing quite a lot of spitting, mostly in Henry's direction. Hester unlocked the River Island grilles and, with Henry and Will, shepherded the two Romanians over to the far wall and the damaged window.

'See ya,' called Henry. 'Wouldn't want to be ya!' Nadia spat at him again. 'Do that once more and I'll knock you out, love.'

Hester was first to realise that the Jaguar was no longer embedded in the window. Getting ahead of Alex and Nadia, he looked outside. Zombies moved in the near distance, but there was no car at all to be seen. He puzzled over why the people outside would come in for it. Will stated the obvious, 'No car.' Then Hester realised where it must be. While he mused over Lee's group having the nerve to pull off such a stunt, Nadia had jumped outside. Alex said something to her, presumably about there being no transport, but she was already off across the car-park, wanting to be away from the nasty English bastard people. Alex jumped down and ran after his sister.

Henry looked to Hester. 'Will they get past the zombies?'

'They're going to have to. Anyway, enough of this. Good riddance to them.'

They left the store and Hester locked it down again.

A couple of hours later, after having lunch with a particularly sullen Cozzie, who he needed to have words with about her attitude, Hester took a climb up into the dome. The rifle was slung over his shoulder by its strap – no longer an unacceptable sight around the mall. Slowly he moved in a circle, taking in the view, despite poor weather and low cloud. He saw the same pall of smoke witnessed by Lee and Madesio. It just reminded him to talk to his people about fire prevention on his American property. Further round, the sun was trying to come out over the town. There were a couple of smaller fires to be seen there. Was it Bonfire night? he thought, or were they well beyond that date? Almost back to the door to the dome he looked down to the car-park, with its forever moving zombies. Then he saw a cluster of bodies halfway to the fence. He could make out the gaudy clothing of Nadia, clearly in distress, pinned to the floor by a zombie, while just beyond that, Alex struggled limply in the grip of two of the machines. It was a pitiable sight, especially as he knew exactly how long it had been going on for.

Hester took another slow tour of the dome while thinking. In the thirty seconds that used up, the situation down there had not improved. His lips pursed as he puzzled over his dilemma. What should he do? Go and help? Go and try to make the people outside help? Go downstairs to Base Camp and ignore it all? He opened one of the windows to stare out across the car-park. There seemed to be a pool of blood underneath the melee. That made his mind up for him. He reached for the rifle, put it through the opening and settled himself on the sill. He concentrated as hard as he could, and put a bullet into Alex's head. Hester let out his breath in a deep sigh. That was for the best, he told himself. It was cruel to let people suffer. He raised the rifle again and took aim on Nadia.

Lee found Claudia in one of the Jon Lewis staff shower cubicles. He had called her name from the door and been happy to wait, but she called him in and popped her head around the shower curtain. She looked beautiful in a different sort of way, with her wet hair flattened to her head.

'What do you want?' she asked, nicely.

'We're playing Monopoly, and Madesio says the pizzas are ready.'

'Saturday night in Berkshire, eh?'

'Is it Saturday night?'

'I've no idea. Do you want to come in?'

'What, with pizza and Monopoly waiting? Are you mad?'

He did at least kiss her. They were both very tempted to have him join her.

'Lee. I've been thinking, you know.'

He looked up and down her soaked arm, right shoulder and at her neck, all that he was going to get of the vision. 'What about?'

'Leila.'

'Leila again?'

'It just doesn't feel right. I know she acts like it doesn't bother her, but she loves you in her own mixed-up kind of way. It must be terrible to see us getting it on, so to speak. Maybe we should cool it until we get out. I know, if we were in the real world, I'd be horrified to have to watch what she has to watch.'

'Claudia, babe, in the real world I never would have been with Leila. It's only because of this strange set-up that it happened at all. You shouldn't think so much.'

She gave him a playful pout. 'I shouldn't think so much?

What is this, Victorian England?'

'Just be happy being my trophy girlfriend.' He made a move. 'What are you like? Come on, spending hours in there. Pizza, Monopoly.'

Lee walked over to where Leila was waiting to play Monopoly. She pulled her iPod ear phones out as he sat down next to her.

'How's my beautiful Ex, then?' he asked.

She smiled, then she shoved the ear phones into his ears. He found himself listening to Adele's *Someone Like You*, while Leila sat back with legs crossed, happily watching him.

Once it had finished, he handed back the iPod. 'I'll never forget you.' He kissed her softly on the lips and got up to help Madesio, arriving with the pizzas.

THIRTY-ONE

The people in Hester's group sat around in Base Camp in silence, with nothing more to say to each other, all of them just begging for the day when some suited and booted strangers would walk in and tell them they were free to go outside the building, to go outside the fence.

Will was virtually comatose, all his teenage energy spent over the past five and a half months.

Tony and Beverley had decided they needed a good talk about Hester's proposals, especially as it seemed that Cathy was going to pull out. She had already put a stop to their fun. From her own viewpoint, Cathy just wished she had gone with Madesio when he asked her to. She was more miserable than when her boyfriend had left her.

Cozzie was very worried. She never realised how much London was in her soul and wanted nothing more than to get back there. Or maybe she didn't like to have to think about what Hester wanted her to do. She still craved his wealth, and felt her life was going to be awful without it, but overall he frightened her to death.

Only Henry was content with his lot. As soon as he got the rest of his money, he would remind Hester of their conversation in the tram tunnel – about his wife and kids back in Manchester. He saw no reason for there to be a problem.

Hester leant across to Cozzie. 'When are you going to move into Ann Summers?'

'That's something I never thought I'd hear. Move in with you? With less than two weeks to go?'

'Start where we mean to carry on in the US. We can have an intense two weeks without any coming and going to Next.'

Cozzie thought what that intense two weeks would be like. She forced herself to say, 'Of course.'

Hester told Will to help Cozzie move into Ann Summers. Will thought that was a stupid idea; he was tired and fed up. He decided he would look into it later in the day – the lazy cow might get her stuff over there on her own. He headed, instead, to his bed for a lie-down.

Hester found Cozzie carrying clothes down the escalator. When he asked if Will was pulling his weight, he saw red at her negative and puzzled answer.

'What do you mean you haven't seen him?'

'I've not seen Will. This is my fifth trip.'

Hester's large head went red. He spun on his heels, his eyes flicking everywhere for Will. The boy presented himself, obviously yawning as he walked towards them. Hester attacked Will, in full view of Cozzie and Tony. He didn't punch him to the ground, he held him up by the throat so he could punch him several times without him annoyingly falling away from him. Cozzie cried out for him to stop, and Tony ran over, but the damage was done – Will was a bloody mess. He sat down where he was on the cold floor, with Cozzie kneeling over him. Hester didn't know where he was. Slowly he recognised Tony, freed himself from the man's concerned grasp and staggered away.

Will was cleaned up by Beverley. He was cut and bruised but not in need of the doctor. Remarkably his general demeanour appeared no different; he didn't want revenge or express a desire to leave, it was all the same to Will. It affected Cozzie more, as well as Cathy when she heard about it. Cozzie was installed in Hester's pokey boudoir for the final stage of their stay. Apart from the man's visits, she had been happy up in Next. She and Cathy didn't discuss what had been done to Will; they just kept looking at each other during the day, and especially over the evening meal.

Finally, when Beverley and Tony were clearing the dishes away, Henry was absent, Will seemed asleep, and Hester went to the gents, Cathy approached Cozzie and quietly asked, 'Shall we go?'

When Cozzie nodded, the two women held hands and ran from the Base Camp. They didn't stop until they reached Jon Lewis, despite being near to collapse and frightened as Will caught them up on his bike and harassed them without actually speaking.

'Hello!' called Cathy, in the middle of the ground floor of Jon Lewis. 'Hello, anyone there?'

Madesio called down, and the two women, near to tears, showed themselves at the bottom of the escalator. Madesio shouted for Lee. They took up the net and admitted the women.

They were sat down and given water. Cozzie had emotionally shut down, leaving it to Cathy to explain the reasons for their flight. 'We're so sorry,' said Cathy. 'Madesio, please forgive me, I should have left there when you asked me. Hester just beat Will up today. It's a terrible situation down there.'

Claudia sat and held Cathy's hands, looking up at Lee. 'Lee, surely it's time to get out of here?'

'Claudia, it's just over a week. That's all. The two ladies stay here with us. We don't leave this floor.'

Claudia struggled to find a way to justify staying. 'Our group came here without too much of a row. They've sort of betrayed the man at the last minute.'

Dr Afridi had an opinion. 'These two ladies would still find it hard to leave early, with or without promise of payment.'

'Can't you call in a medical emergency?' asked Claudia.

'Well, they didn't actually tell me how to go about doing that.'

'Oh, that's great. So we stay holed up here?'

Cozzie suddenly flared up. 'I want the money the bastard promised me. I'm not leaving this building early.'

'Okay,' said Lee. 'Let's get through to the end.'

The nets were put back down the escalator, as well as a few extra pieces of furniture. Cozzie and Cathy were settled in by Claudia and Leila.

Lee and Madesio went into conference; they had their knives and baseball bats, nobody could come up the escalators without them knowing, they had enough food and water stocked in. What could Hester do to them, even assuming that he wanted to do anything?

GB Hope

THIRTY-TWO

Hester and Will crept away from Base Camp while it was still dark. They walked through the mall, heading towards Jon Lewis. As they passed through the shop's entranceway, Hester took a good look at the remains of the half-zombie – nobody had told him about that one.

They skirted away from the two escalators and entered the staff area on the ground floor. As stealthily as possible, they walked up the back stairs until they could approach the doors into where Lee and his people were sleeping. They peered through round meshed windows in the doors, everywhere apparently quiet.

'Right here will do,' said Hester.

From his pockets, Will brought four rags, which were soaked in paraffin. He pressed them against the base of the doors. Hester was already striking three matches in one go, which he dropped on top of the rags. There wasn't an instantly huge conflagration but the fire would clearly take hold. Hester dragged over some cardboard boxes and two foam-filled swivel chairs to add to the fire, just to make sure.

'Out,' said Hester quietly, patting Will on the shoulder.

They left the way they had come in, with orange light

flickering onto their backs. They departed Jon Lewis without being heard. Will knew what they had just done was terribly wrong but he was still massively keyed up by it, making faces and blowing out air like a sprinter with adrenalin already coursing his veins at the start line. He never saw the blow to the back of the head which knocked him out cold.

Will came round in a prone position, extremely comfortable and warm, as if he had taken a fall and now found himself in a lovely hospital bed. But then he found that he was bound and gagged, strapped into something highly unusual. In a panic, he thrashed around and turned his head from side to side to see where he was.

He was in the virtual bungee jump machine. At first he thought, what a silly place to keep him prisoner. Was it just the straps in the apparatus to tie him with that had made it seem a sensible idea? Then he realised that the machine was warming up. The floor beneath him turned blue to represent the river scene. Up went the gyroscope machine and he began being put through the bungee jump sensation. He kept his eyes closed, but the feeling was all-encompassing and made his heart want to burst from his chest. The ride came to an end. If he could have, he would have shouted "very funny, get me off now!" To his horror the machine was dipping him forward for another go. 'No!' he screamed through his gag.

In the control cubicle, Hester made sure that the machine was stuck on "repeat process", then slipped out of the shop, without Will seeing him.

At last! thought Lee, the dream had finally come to him – Claudia, Leila and himself all in the same bed. And it was turning vigorous as well, Claudia to his left side, with Leila taking her turn on top of him. He strained to kiss Claudia, grateful for her understanding, while caressing Leila's slim, gyrating hips.

'Lee! Wake up!'

It all turned frantic, he awoke into confusion.

'Lee!' It was a different voice. Claudia and Leila were both on at him. 'There's a fire!'

Now he was fully awake, jumping to his knees, seeing terror in Leila's face. He felt Claudia grab him. The room seemed smaller in the dark, and he realised black smoke was moving across the ceiling. 'Let's get out! Where's it coming from?'

'The back,' said Claudia, fear in her voice.

'Escalators! Go!'

He pulled the two girls out of the art gallery, trying to see the way between furniture. The white nightshirt of Dr Afridi moved into view.

'Doctor, where are the others?'

'Madesio's getting them.'

They got to the escalator and Lee started hauling on the nets, but they were jammed with the extra furniture. By then Claudia and Leila were coughing.

'Climb down!' Lee ordered them.

Claudia went first, stumbling down through the netting. Leila followed. Madesio arrived, dragging a distraught Cozzie and Cathy, both in their day-old pyjamas. Lee pushed them both in the direction the other two girls had gone. He looked over his shoulder, seeing an orange glow beyond the black billowing smoke.

As Madesio followed Dr Afridi down, and as Lee prepared to depart also, the sprinkler system kicked in throughout the store. It was a serious downpour, which instantly soaked them all. It upset the terrified women at the bottom of the escalator even more. Before he started to climb down, Lee looked back again. The orange glare of the fire had gone, the sprinklers were doing their job.

Completely saturated and freezing, the seven of them hurried out of the store into the dry concourse. Madesio turned to face Lee, calm in himself but unsure of where to go. Lee put a hand on the back of the American's neck. 'I think it's well under control up there. It's raining outside, we need proper clothes if we're going out.' They both looked at the nearest stores on the Blade. 'I'll go back and check that the fire's out. Wait here for a minute.'

Lee returned up the blocked escalator, slipping twice in the wetness, with smoke billowing around him, but it was more of a nuisance than a danger, and lessening with every second. At the top he was able to witness the water-ruined store. Then the sprinklers began to cease. He walked about until he was satisfied that wherever the fire had started, it was now out.

Back downstairs, Madesio told Lee which store they needed to go in. 'We'll get everyone dry,' he said. 'And check for a fire exit.'

'Okay, Madesio.'

They shepherded the bedraggled survivors into a store. Last one in, Lee did a double-take, stepped back outside and read the name of the store: HESTER'S FABRICS. Shaking his head in disbelief, he joined the others, stripping off and towelling down. Dr Afridi tried to keep some decorum by gesturing for the other men to turn away like himself from the naked females.

They all ended up in dressing gowns. Lee went round all the girls to see if they were all right. They all seemed non the worse for the experience.

They decided to spend the night in Hester's Fabrics, with there being enough leather couches to sleep on and luxurious fabrics to act as blankets. Lee and Madesio shared the night watch duties. By the time the sun was streaming into the North Blade, they were all awake, in various stages of disorientation. Lee gave Claudia a big hug. Part of him wanted to do the same to Leila, but he didn't. Lee, carrying a wooden curtain rail as a weapon, then accompanied Dr Afridi and Cathy to search out breakfast for everyone.

With food inside them, everyone fully recovered from the night's drama. Not wanting to split the group, Lee led them all back up into Jon Lewis to assess the damage. They clambered up over the nets and looked about them. Mainly it was the same problem as when the early flood ruined parts of the downstairs stores. Plus, the air was rank with the smell of smoke. In the rear, the staff area was gutted out and blackened.

'Could we come back in here?' asked Cathy. 'If we got new bedding?'

Lee looked at Dr Afridi, who was shaking his head.

'Everyone, stay here. I'll go and find a store where we can

control the shutters. Then we'll get new beds and supplies in there, and sit out the final days. Is that all right?'

They all nodded. Lee said to Madesio, 'Look after them, I'll be back as quick as I can.'

Lee found his knife under the soaked bed in the art gallery, then went downstairs to examine all the stores along the North Blade. He just knew it would happen – the only store where he found the key to the security grille was Hester's Fabrics. They would have to set up camp in there.

THIRTY-THREE

The decision was made not to bother finding new beds, as the wide sofas in Hester's Fabrics were perfectly comfortable. They gathered them together into a little commune near the fire exit which was hidden from the entrance by all the fabrics and soft furnishings. There were two windows, floor to ceiling ones of thick glass, like the kind you see in council buildings or libraries. It was carpeted throughout and fairly cosy.

Lee accepted that there would be no further hanky panky with Claudia until the end came, not that anyone was thinking along those lines, and besides, he was sharing the night watch with Madesio. Everyone just occupied the space, talking and eating. If they had known how many days were left, they would have been counting them. At one stage they tried to pass a few hours telling jokes. Claudia told the Billy Connolly one about the tramp on the bus, forcing Billy to have a sweet, with the punch line "that's been up my arse". They all fell about after that one. It was Lee's turn, 'My grandparents were called Pearl and Dean. But we just called them Ma and Pa, Pa, Pa, Pa, Pa, Pa, Pa, Pa – Pa, Pa, Pa.' Everyone laughed, apart from Leila who didn't get it at all.

'It's a tune that used to be played in the cinema before the film came on,' explained Claudia.

Leila wanted to get it even less.

Naturally, Cathy and Cozzie were questioned about life in the other group. They explained how the mood had deteriorated with Hester becoming more and more controlling, not in an overtly aggressive way, apart from when he beat up Will, but just the manner in which he continually attempted to impose his way of doing things. Cozzie neglected to mention her probationary period as the man's mistress. When Cathy answered questions about Beverley and Tony, she also kept quiet about her love triangle. Lee and Madesio, the late night Waterstones raiders, exchanged a glance.

'Hester made the Romanians leave,' said Cozzie.

'Leave?' asked Lee. 'Leave how?'

'Well, the cutting of Beverley's arm was the last straw. He, Henry and Will threw them out. Made them leave in the car they arrived in.'

Lee looked at Madesio again.

Madesio let Lee out of Hester's Fabrics, then locked the grille down again after him. 'I'll be quick as I can,' Lee told him. He went through Jon Lewis and watchfully stepped out through the fire exit. It was all clear. The Jaguar was where they had left it. Next, he went up onto the roof. It was nice to see Leila and Claudia's sun loungers and the abandoned copy of *A Touch of Frost*. It made him smile. Less pleasant was the smoke rising from his pen-pal's house outside the fence. He stopped and stared at it, extremely disturbed, wondering what on earth it could mean.

Tearing his eyes away, he moved along the roof in the direction of the central dome, seeing those fucking zombies still wandering around. He wondered if they stopped at night and were recharged by technicians – in a type of *Westworld* film set-up.

Then he saw something which he couldn't quite make out, and yet, in his mind he knew exactly what it was. A mangle of shapes lay in a black stain on the car park. Three silenced zombies were entwined with the bodies of Alex and Nadia. Lee looked out there for a long time.

'Madesio, where the fuck are they!?'

After his run back down, he found that Leila and Cathy were absent from the store.

'The john's blocked up back there,' explained Madesio, 'They had to go to the Ladies.'

All the others gathered at the sound of Lee's distressed voice. He spun round and ran off, calling back, 'Madesio, find yourself a knife!'

He checked the public lavatories on the North Blade but failed to find them. He started to run in and out of the shops, panic and adrenalin making his body sweat more than just through the exertion. In the adventure store he stopped running as he saw images of light flashing on the ceiling and a little mechanical noise. He moved towards the centre of the shop, towards the virtual bungee compartment. He glanced in slowly; the machine was definitely on. The lifeless body of Will suspended upside down in the contraption almost made him throw up. Will's face was hideously bloated with blood beneath the skin and his eyes were almost out of their sockets. Lee managed to reach out and touch the boy's neck in search of a pulse but it was clearly a hopeless gesture. He backed out of there.

Then, outside, he heard the girls running towards him from an annex corridor. His heart emptied horribly when he realised it was Cathy alone, highly upset and panting for air.

'Hester's taken her!' she screamed into his face as he held her. 'Hester's taken Leila! He just slapped me aside and put her over his shoulder. Oh, Lee!'

Lee was already dragging her by the arm back to Hester's Fabrics. He virtually threw her into Cozzie's arms, then grabbed Madesio by the front of his shirt and said, 'Alex and Nadia, dead on the car park. Do you understand me?' He gestured to the frightened group, watching on, it dawning on them that something terrible had occurred. 'Get them out, Madesio. Get them out.'

'Okay, man. And you?'

'I'm going after Leila.'

Lee embraced Claudia firmly. 'He's taken Leila,' he whispered to her ear.

'Lee, what's happened?'

'Hester's murdered the Romanians.' She gasped. 'Go with Madesio. I'll meet you out in the town.'

'My God, Lee. We'll get the police. That's what we'll do, we'll get the police.'

'I have to go for her now. I will find you, Claudia. I will find you.'

She was nodding. They kissed before he let her go and

hurried from the store.

Madesio led Dr Afridi and the three women out via Jon Lewis. Cozzie was crying and being comforted by Cathy. Once outside, they had a clear run to the Jaguar. 'Women in the back,' called Madesio. They all clambered in and Madesio turned the engine over, without success. He kept trying and kept failing, adding to Cozzie's misery. Finally the engine caught, the noise synchronising with that of a zombie smashing his head through the back window, all the girls screaming. Madesio fumbled for reverse gear, managed to find it and the Jag flew backwards, continuing on until it rammed the zombie into the wall of Jon Lewis. They were then faced with a group of the things bearing down on them.

Lee moved towards Base Camp. He was angry, raging even, but not feeling particularly brave. He touched the knife at his back, like a homeowner disturbed by a burglar – could he actually stick it in someone? He realised his pumping heart was interfering with his decision-making, not thinking where exactly he needed to go. He thought of his real father, who once tackled a mugger without losing his composure even slightly. He must be like his father, he told himself. Do what has to be done but keep your mind switched on.

He heard bicycle brakes on the upper level. He thought it was Will, then remembered the horrible way in which the lad had died. He ignored the sound and strained to see across the far-off Base Camp. It seemed empty. The cyclist appeared at the top of the escalator: it was Henry.

'Henry! For fuck's sake! Do you know what's happening

here? Come on!'

Henry dismounted and discarded Will's bike. He had lost touch with reality; all he saw was this troublemaker trying to interfere with what was due to him and his family. He brought his own knife into view, something which terrified Lee. Still, Lee walked up the adjoining escalator, never taking his eyes off Henry. Henry approached Lee as he reached the top. He came on cautiously, not allowing the smaller man another chance to take him to the ground. Lee withdrew his own blade. There was no turning back. He had nothing more to say to Henry, just showing him the blade as they closed up – showing it, showing it, making him look at it, then lashing out instead with a right foot kick to Henry's left calf that clearly hurt the man. Furious to be duped again, Henry slashed back and forth for Lee's face, who jumped back. Lee was thinking fast, trying to recall his father's lesson's about dealing with a knife attack. The only manoeuvre he remembered involved grabbing the knife hand and twisting it – sorry, dad, that didn't count for much here. There was another flurry of blades and a metallic sound that time. Lee kicked for Henry's head, missed and swore at himself for risking injury. His dad would keep it simple in a real fight.

Henry was concerned with the martial arts stuff coming at him. He wanted to finish it quickly, as if he was outside a Manchester pub. He lunged, ran even, at Lee. The knives pinged again. He was surprised that neither of them had been cut in that clash, and while he was thinking that, for that split-second, the kick came from Lee, with power only found in adrenalin-fuelled fear, right to his chest and he was gone, backwards over the banister to the marble floor below.

GB Hope

THIRTY-FOUR

The Jag had rammed a few zombies with a burst of initial energy and headed off across the car-park. But then it wasn't well at all, crawling along at about 3 mph. with steam rising from the bonnet. Halfway to the gate, with the smoke from the house acting as a homing beacon, it finally gave up the ghost and spluttered to a stop. Everyone in the car chose a different window to watch approaching zombies from.

A far away scream dragged Lee from the trance of staring down at Henry's lifeless body. He put his knife back in his belt and moved along the upper level until he was above Base Camp. The sound of gunfire echoed around the rooftop, forcing his attention up to the dome. His brain was frozen again. He was trying to remember how to get high up in the building when a stooped figure coming out of the door to the crystal feature showed him the way. It was Andrew Scholes, the squatter, who stood up straight and looked him in the face.

'Scholes! Why are you still here? Can't you hear the shooting? Get the hell out!'

From within his tramp's coat, Scholes brought out a

pistol and fired at Lee. At that exact split second, Lee had turned away and upwards towards the sound of another scream, so the bullet took away the left corner of his mouth instead of entering his head through his left cheekbone. Scholes fired again, but had a jammed weapon in his hand. In instant agony and with blood spraying over his left shoulder and chest, Lee had his knife out and thrown at Scholes, simultaneously running forward. The knife hit Scholes by the handle, around the Adam's apple, but it was enough to allow Lee to close the gap. Left and right punches came up with expert twisting of the hips for maximum power, with Scholes almost out on his feet. Lee, who did his best work on the floor, swept Scholes' legs from under him and got the man in a choke hold. As his blood leaked onto Scholes' unshaven face, the bleeding made worse by his terrible exertion, there was nobody there that time to make Lee stop. When Scholes went limp, he let him fall to the side.

Madesio made Dr Afridi and the girls push the Jag while he kept turning the ignition key. If he got it going again he would need it to ram the gate. Thankfully, the zombie threat had moved away, because they were currently methodically tracking after Beverley and Tony, who were attempting to flee on foot. Then the shooting started, from somewhere up high. Zombies were hit and disabled, but the shots were not in defence of the Yorkshire couple, they were at them, bullets hitting the concrete at their feet as they scuttled in search of safety. The people at the car saw Beverley hit, with a spurt of blood from her shoulder and a lifeless collapse.

Tony fell to his knees beside his wife. The shooting paused. The zombies closed in.

Madesio felt the car engine roar into life. With just thirty feet to go he gunned it away from the others and slammed into the gate. The Jag rolled back, completely finished. Madesio got out to see a gap in the fence. He waved for the others and they stepped off the car-park.

Lee was completely zoned out by then – two murders in one day. No thoughts of manslaughter or reasonable force could enter his traumatised subconscious, he just felt like a killer. The man Scholes, he thought, must have been Hester's sleeper, planted there amongst them for if everything went to hell. He ripped part of his shirt that wasn't bloody and had it sticking out of his mouth. His blood loss wasn't too bad, considering how it had been caused. He entered the stairwell to the dome, to a girl's cry – Leila. He went up quickly, realising he didn't have a weapon, so turned all gung-ho to have a crack at Hester straight away.

It was a scene of madness that met him up in the dome. Leila was next to Hester, clearly with her hands tied behind her back, her terrified eyes pleading for Lee's help. Hester had the rifle through the window with one arm while holding Leila with the other. On sensing Lee's presence he pushed back and swung the barrel of the rifle to aim at Lee. But he didn't fire, maybe believing he needed to reload. Instead, he started to mount the metal ladder to the roof, dragging a screaming Leila after him by her collar, almost ripping her shirt over her head and revealing her slim abdomen.

Lee could do nothing but follow. It was gusty up there. The wind turbine moved noisily around. Lee knew he had to get rid of that rifle – he had used up his luck for that lifetime downstairs with Scholes. Leila struggled. Hester seemed more concerned with the weapon. Lee gambled that it was, indeed, unloaded and made a move. Hester discarded Leila like an empty cigarette packet, now free to swing the rifle at Lee. Lee took the blow to his ribcage as his fee to get in close. He punched Hester on the chin, without much effect. He punched again to the stomach. Big man Hester took it and grappled with Lee, the rifle entangled but hanging useless. Lee took hits to his head, and especially painful punches to the left of his face. He couldn't get Hester down. He knew he could have him if he could only get him down. They were like two sumo wrestlers trying to get the upper hand. Gradually, Hester had his man over towards the edge. He was grasping for a neck hold with one hand so he could deliver big punches with the other.

Lee heard screaming, in such dire straits he thought it might have been coming from himself. Hester got that neck hold, Lee felt his strength going, punches still raining in. Lee felt he was going 7 and 2 in his fight career. One more massive blow came from Hester's fist. Lee was nearly gone, over the edge. Then Hester suddenly gave up the fight. Lee thought the man must have had a heart attack, or something. Obviously, in the wind and the violent tussling, he had not heard the shot that went through Hester's right temple and took most of the back of his head off. Hester toppled backwards and fell from the roof, with the turbine blades seeming to wave him off.

Lee sank to his knees and looked at Leila. But she had not killed Hester with the rifle. She was still bound and crying pitifully. Lee turned his eyes and saw a swarthy stranger halfway out of the hatch, a pistol in his hands. Then he must have passed out.

As Lee came round, he realised he was lying on the floor of the dome. He struggled to focus his eyes and saw Leila hugging a man nearby – she's moved on quickly, he thought. He managed to sit himself up. Leila rushed over to him and caressed the undamaged side of his face.

'Are you all right, Lee?' she asked. 'It's over now. Your face is a right mess, you know.'

'Thanks for that.'

She kissed his right cheek as if they were still a couple. Lee was more interested in finding out who the man was. He stood there all in black, curly dark hair, unshaven. The handgun was no longer in view.

'Lee, let me introduce my brother, Musa. He's come here to find me.'

'Thank God for that,' mumbled Lee, through his swelling face.

Musa came close to examine Lee's wound. 'I've seen worse, my friend. You'll have a sexy scar.'

Never mind that, thought Lee, how about an ambulance? Or the police?

'Can you get up?' asked Musa.

'If I have to.'

Lee stood up. He looked through the windows. It was a shock to look at the nearby town – almost every house seemed to be ablaze with black smoke rising to the sky. 'What the hell's happening out there?'

'All in good time,' said Musa. 'Can you walk? We'll clean you up, get you some water.'

With Leila holding his hand, Lee was led down the stairs and into Base Camp. He was sat down. Musa briefly went away, coming back with a bottle of water and a new shirt for Lee. While he gingerly changed, Lee watched Musa affectionately touch his sister's chin.

'How did you find me?' Leila asked her brother.

'The London man. No, don't worry, I left him in good health.'

Musa came over to squat in front of Lee.

'You're my sister's friend,' said Musa. 'I thank you with all my heart for coming to save her. We must leave this place now.'

Leila took Lee's hand again and they left the mall through the entrance where it had all started so many months ago. Smoke was visible all around the horizon. Musa clicked open the central locking of a Land Rover Discovery. He turned to Lee.

'Well?' asked Lee. 'Tell me what's happened.'

'The world has exploded, my friend. Violence and rioting – every village, every town, every city. Through most of Europe, as far as we know.'

'But why?'

Musa shrugged, not a man given to making speeches. 'Collapse of banks, fall of governments, no fuel, no jobs. Chaos came, my friend, while you and my sister were playing games in there.'

Lee thought of his loved ones, but there was no point in talking to Musa about individual places. He got into the back of the Land Rover with Leila, who reclaimed his hand, and Musa drove them slowly around the building. Lee looked at the pale yellow brickwork, with one deep red smudge where Hester had ricocheted on his way down. Instead of looking at Hester's body, Lee glanced up at the dome, with the still turning wind turbine. They skirted several zombies and tried not to look at the other corpses. Musa forced the Land Rover through the opening made by the Jaguar, then stopped the vehicle and turned off the engine.

The others stood there, clearly unsure about heading into the Berkshire town. Lee got out of the Land Rover to receive Claudia running to his arms. She would have kissed him but for his wounded face.

'Lee, you're hurt!'

'It's not too bad, apparently,' he mumbled at her. 'According to Leila's brother there.'

Claudia looked across at the man. 'Leila's brother? Lee, thank God you're safe.' She settled for a deep hug. 'Can we go home now?'

Lee held her out in front of him, to enjoy looking at her beautiful face, but he didn't know what to say to her. He pulled Claudia back to his chest. Beyond strands of her hair blowing in the breeze, he looked off towards the town. After a moment, he released her. He looked at the nearest house, the home from which he thought he had communicated with the man on the roof – it was a burnt out shell. There was a terrible smell in the air, and not just from the burning buildings – looking back to the town he could see dozens of bodies lying on the ground, and they were not pretend zombies.

Musa was very keen to go. Lee stared at the man, then took Claudia's hand and they all squeezed into the Land Rover. Leila's brother drove them slowly out through the sacked town.